Unassailable

Book Three in the "Casts of Silver" Series

K.J. ROWE

Ark House Press
arkhousepress.com

Cataloguing in Publication Data:
Title: Unassailable
Series: Casts of Silver Series, Book 3
ISBN: 978-0-6457514-1-3 (pbk)
Subjects: Fiction
Other Authors/Contributors: Rowe, K.J.
Design by initiateagency.com

"…let us throw off everything that hinders and the sin that so easily entangles. And let us run with perseverance with race marked out for us."
Hebrews 12:1b (NIV)

ONE

Hope Meyer slumped into the window seat of her bedroom, looking out the window at a neighborhood bathed in the cool blue light of the full moon. She would have been thrilled to hear of Lexi and Dylan becoming a couple less than a year ago, so why wasn't she so thrilled now?

Hope turned the phone over in her hands and replayed the conversation with Lexi in her mind. Her best mate was babbling with details, and there were moments Hope had to ask her to repeat herself. Hope had laughed along and gushed at the right moments, but her heart sank lower and lower until Lexi had to go. Because Dylan was on the other line …

Dylan.

What was it about Dylan that she admired?

She didn't know. Her opinion of him had changed in her sight since she'd seen him go into bat for Lexi. The way he flew at Brad, the way he cared for Lexi, the way he restrained himself until she was ready for a relationship. It was all so appealing.

But why?

The ugly twinge of jealousy twisted in her gut again, and she groaned. With a flick of her hand, she tossed the phone on the bed and moved to her dressing table. She sat and looked over the pictures of models and actresses she had pinned around the mirror, then looked at her reflection. Hair and makeup always made her feel better. Maybe she could add some cinnamon highlights to her blond bob? Or sleek it instead of wearing it tousled? Cut in a fringe, perhaps?

The fringe thought inspired Hope and she picked up a comb to test the look when angry voices started up downstairs. With a roll of her eyes, Hope stood and shut her bedroom door. Her parents shouting matches were wearing thin, but it was all they seemed to do of late. Mum hated Dad's new job, and she lost her temper every time he had to go away for the project his firm was working on.

Hope had just retaken her seat in front of the mirror when a rap at her door drew an exasperated sigh from her. "Yeah?"

The bedroom door clicked open, and Ryan poked his head in. "Josh just rocked up after footy training. He's waiting downstairs for you."

Hope's hand tightened on the comb and her lips pressed into a thin line. She gave Ryan a tight smile and rose from her dressing table as he disappeared down the hall. Josh. Josh and his old-fashioned manners. He had always said it wasn't right for him to be in her room, that it would cause others to question her virtue, and he didn't want that for her. They'd been a couple for almost eight months now, and while he didn't call himself a Christian, he embodied everything she was looking for in a Christian man. She'd just have to keep inviting him to come to church and pray he'd come one day.

The house was peaceful once more as Hope made her way downstairs. She followed the sounds of animated conversation that floated down the hall from the kitchen and smiled to herself. Josh only had to appear to settled her parents' argument and bring laughter from them both. Rounding the corner into the kitchen, she found Josh seated at the bench and showing great interest in a story her mum was telling. Genuine interest. That was just the type of guy he was. Gave everyone 100% of his attention.

"Hello, handsome," Hope said when her mum paused to take a breath. "What brings you over this evening? I thought you'd have gone straight home after footy training."

The way his face lit up when he looked at her, brightened her smile as she stopped beside him. His arm encircled her waist, and he tucked her into his side. "Where else would I rather be?"

"We better leave you two kids to it." Dad moved to leave the room. Mum followed, pausing at the mouth of the hallway. "Hope, can you please lock up before you go to bed?"

Hope gave a wave of her hand while continuing to gaze at Josh. He was so boyishly handsome. She loved his caved-in cheeks and strong jawline and how they drew attention to his smile. He had such a great smile, a cheeky smile that brightened her mood even on her darkest days. Even though the heady rushes had faded, she still wanted to be near him. "Well, now you're here and everyone has gone to bed, what did you want to do?"

Josh took one of Hope's hands and entwined his fingers with hers. "Let's have a talk." Josh pulled out another stool at the bench and gestured to it.

A weight suddenly formed in Hope's gut. A guy talk meant only one of two things—a proposal or a break-up—and she wasn't ready for either. His coffee-colored eyes traveled her face in his kind and gentle manner, but her nerves wouldn't still.

"What's up?" Hope tried for a casual tone as she sat before him.

"Why do you want to be with me?"

Hope blinked. "Huh?"

"Why do you want to be with me?" Josh asked again, his voice mild and unhurried while he toyed with her fingers.

Hope swallowed, confused. She squinted back at him, unsure how to answer his question. She blurted out the first sentence her brain formed. "Are you breaking up with me?"

Josh breathed out a soft chuckle and dropped his gaze. With a shake of his head, he looked back at her. "I wouldn't put it quite like that."

Hope snatched back her hand. "Well, what is it then?"

Josh remained calm as he rested his hands on his thighs and continued to look back at her. Hope's nerves grew taut and a heat behind her eyes stung as she searched his face.

"I guess I'm asking, what do you want?" Josh asked quietly. "Because I get the distinct feeling it's not me."

"Why on earth would you think that?"

"The change that came over you not long after Dylan started playing AFL was a big hint."

Hope straightened on her seat, pulling back from Josh. "I don't care about Dylan."

"He told me you were all over him at a church social recently. Not to mention the disaster the birthday party I planned for you turned out to be because Dylan couldn't be there. You sulked the whole night and refused to eat anything. It was embarrassing."

With a dismissive sniff, Hope looked away.

"But that isn't the only thing that has me questioning things," Josh continued. "The way you are with the other players at club functions … sometimes I get asked if we're still together."

"By Max, I bet." Hope couldn't help the snarl that crinkled her nose as she looked back at him.

Josh held a hand up. "It doesn't matter who said what, but yes, he's one of them."

Hope locked her jaw. She could feel herself begin to boil inside, and while one part of her wanted to defend herself, she knew he had a right to speak his mind. But it was his peaceful demeanor that scared her. He'd made his decision, and no conversation was going to change it. She was fighting a losing battle.

"It's not just those things. You say I have old-fashioned values and morals and I know this frustrates you. I'm not going to change. It's how my parents raised me—"

"And that's fine with me—"

"Really? Because sometimes I get the distinct impression you want me to cross the line."

Heat pooled into Hope's face, and she sat back in her seat, both embarrassed and speechless. All she could do was stare back at him. Why on earth would he think that?

Josh reached out and took her hand. "This is why I'm confused, why I'm not sure where I stand with you. I think you need time to sort out whatever is in your head before we can continue. If it's me you want, show me. If it's this God you keep talking to me about, show Him. I guess I just need you to be real."

Hope swallowed what felt like a melon as she looked up at the ceiling. She would not cry. She. would. Not. Cry! "So, you are breaking up with me."

Josh rose and drew her off her seat, wrapping her in an embrace. Against her will, she clung to him as her eyes overflowed.

"No, sweetheart. I'm not," Josh replied huskily, "I'm not going after anybody else. I don't want anybody else. I just think you need some time."

"So I have no choice in this?" Hope whispered against Josh's shirt, stalling the inevitable. She couldn't bear for him to walk out tonight with things as they were. She knew she'd behaved terribly recently but didn't understand why. She'd said things and done things she wasn't proud of, and he didn't deserve it. But surely, she could have a chance to make things right, right?

She looked away as he moved back from her. His hands slipped down her arms and held her hands as he tried to meet her eyes.

"Hope, look at me."

Hope raised her eyes up to him and she hoped he could see the pain he'd caused within their depths. Soft as a whisper, Josh traced his thumb down a tear track on her cheek, and a flicker of anguish cross his features. Had he changed his mind?

Josh shook his head. "No. I've been thinking a lot about this, and I'm making this decision for both of us. If you want to call our relationship over, let me know. As for me, you're still my girl and hopefully will remain so. But I want to be your guy, not your backup. Not the guy you're going out with until someone better comes along."

Hope let out a defeated breath and slumped in her seat. A deep sadness wove its way into her bones at learning how he felt. Tomorrow would start without being able to call him her boyfriend, and no amount of talking would change that.

TWO

Hope dumped each coat hanger she emptied into the box beside her, filling the small change room she was working in with a physical and audible display of her mood.

The ladies wear department of House and Home within the Bridgeshore Plaza had been Hope's job for just over four years. At first, she had been on the checkouts, but managers decided she would be better as floor staff. After trying a few different areas of the store, they settled her in ladies' wear.

Hope tugged a stubborn shirt off a hanger, then discarded both into their respective boxes before slumping back into her chair. She rubbed her eyes and yawned. It had been a bad move to sit up until four in the morning to finish the book she was reading, but she couldn't put it down—plus it took her mind off Josh. Unlike her, the book's heroine had a guy who fought for her.

Like Dylan did for Lexi.

Why didn't Josh fight for her?

She stood and reached for the next garment, wrestling with another tangled shirt strap before disengaging the straps from the hanger. She knew she should pray but nothing came. There was a storm cloud in her mind and a tightness in her gut. It annoyed her that Josh questioned her relationship with God. What would he know? Despite several invitations, he had never come to church with her, so what made him think he could question her when they were out having fun with others?

Fun. Did Josh know the meaning of the word?

"Girlfriend, you are making one hell of a noise in here!"

Hope took a long breath in through her nose and flicked her hair out of her face before turning to look at her colleague. "Sorry, Claudia. I'm in a grump."

"Yeah, I could tell. So could any customers nearby." Claudia perched on the dressing room bench, ankles crossed as she swung her legs and looked back at her. "Get it off your chest now, or Rob will bust in here soon and give us his 'when you come to work, leave your personal life at the door' speech again."

Hope scoffed loudly as she remembered that speech. Rob Halstead, the middle-aged floor manager, was seemingly in a constant bad mood. No one did anything to his satisfaction, and his glare could melt ice. He'd made her cry once, and Hope hadn't been able to stomach the man since. She turned on her seat to face Claudia.

"I finished my novel and had to come back to reality," Hope eventually offered.

Claudia sniffed as a grin curled on her face. "I hate that, too. But I'm sure that's not the whole story. Has it got something to do with Josh?

A frown crossed Hope's brow. "Why do you say that?"

"Because last night would have been a footy training night, and you're grumpy this morning. So something would have happened last night with him." Claudia picked up a notepad from beside her and took a pen out of her hair bun. "I'm going to guess it's about that Max guy. Pass me that box of clothes beside you, please."

Hope pushed the box of clothes over to her workmate. "Why would I be in a grump over Max?" A niggle of guilt tickled her mind. Josh had mentioned Max last night.

Claudia smirked. "Because from all the stories you tell me about club functions—after-training gatherings, game days, and all that nonsense—Max seems a little smooth."

A grin tugged on the corner of Hope's mouth. Max Mason. The Tigers full forward she'd suspected had been keen on her from the first time they'd met. As she'd spent more time around the club, she'd decided that was just how he was. Playful. Same as she was. Neither of them meant anything by it, but Josh seemed to think there was more.

"Yes, Max is smooth. But he's also the club clown, and I love having fun. We bounce off each other well. I think Josh is a bit touchy—you know how some guys are? We've had words over it before."

Claudia opened the box Hope had given her and hummed as she sifted through the items inside. "I wouldn't be so sure. It sounds to me like Max is sweet on you, and who knows what locker room talk is going on. I bet Josh sees it differently."

Before Hope could answer, a customer service bell chimed, and Claudia stabbed her bun with the pen and jumped off the counter to answer the call. With a lift of her shoulder, Hope picked up the box of coat hangers to head out the back to the storage room. Claudia had no idea what she was talking about. There was no way Max was sweet on Hope.

Hope hip- bumped the storage room doors open and backed into the cool quiet room, maneuvering the cumbersome box along with her.

"Need a hand with that?"

Hope grinned at the sound of Scott Kinton's gravelly voice somewhere behind her.

"Reckon I've got it covered, thanks." With a grunt, she pitched the box onto a vacant shelf to her right. Dusting her hands off, she turned to Scott. "Thanks for the offer. What are you doing out the back?"

Scott grinned at her, his stylus poised over the tablet in his hand. "Stocktaking. What are you working on? By the way, you should have used two smaller boxes for that job. If Rob saw that, he'd put you in safe work practices training again."

Hope hung her hands off her hips. "Don't get me started on Rob."

"I won't." Scott moved a box to the side before scribbling another note. "Everyone knows you two hate each other. He's probably waiting for an opportunity to fire you."

Hope swallowed. Scott was right. Rob had been her manager for the last two years, and they had clashed the entire time. Rob didn't like her, and she couldn't figure out why. Everyone else liked her. Maybe what made matters worse was that he didn't like that whatever the new department supervisor, Liam Clacey, asked her to do overrode what he asked her to do? Well, you could catch more flies with honey, and Liam was nicer to her. Much nicer.

"Yeah, he'll have to beat me to the punch. I'm not going to be around here for much longer."

Scott turned to her; his eyebrows raised as he slid the stylus back into the tablet. "You quitting?"

"I'm not going to work here my whole life, am I?" Hope dropped her eyes and picked at her fingernails. When Scott didn't say anything, she looked up.

His expression said it all. He leaned against the wall and crossed his arms. His brown eyes held a laugh, and the smile he was restraining only deepened his dimples as he looked back at her. Hope straightened.

"What? Did you think I was aiming to climb the management ladder here or something?"

"Not at all." Scott chuckled. A moment of silence passed between them while Hope held his eyes. She didn't want to insult him in case he had decided to climb the management ladder himself while he continued studying at uni. She was about to correct herself, when he broke the silence.

"Okay. I'll bite. What's your plan? You know I'm headed back to the family farm as soon as I've finished my Bachelor of Agriculture. What's your plan?"

"Plan?" A frown crossed Hope's brow as she took in Scott's amused expression. "I don't need a plan to quit my job. I've had enough, so I want out. Why does everyone think I need something?" She heard the snipy tone in her voice as Josh's words flashed into her mind. Hope shook her head and waved a hand at Scott's surprised expression. "Sorry about that. I'm just tired. I mean, I'm not sure what I'm going to do. All I know is it doesn't involve this place."

"Alright then. That's cool." Scott pulled out the stylus from the tablet in his hand and turned to the shelves next to him. "You still coming to Gavin's party on Saturday night?"

Hope smiled back at Scott as he glanced over his shoulder at her. "Yes. Wouldn't miss it. Well, I better get back to work before Rob comes after me. Don't overdo it out here."

Scott gave a tap to an imaginary hat. "No, ma'am. Catchya."

Hope pushed through the storeroom doors with a parting smile back at Scott before the heavy doors closed behind her. She loved Scott's country boy roots that came out from time to time. It always made her feel like she was in a Hallmark movie. With a skip in her step, Hope headed back to the changerooms to finish the list of jobs Rob had left the afternoon staff.

As she buried herself in the list of jobs, Scott's question about her future plans bothered her. How did everyone else find out what they wanted to do? Did they always know, or did it fall in their lap somehow?

God, help me find what you want me to do. Surely, it's not working here at the plaza forever. Do I go back to school? Do I apply for another job somewhere? And what do I do about Josh? I miss him so much.

Help me.

THREE

"Hope, you can't avoid food prep. It's something we all have to help with as youth group leaders."

Hope looked up from a study of her nails and over the island bench to where Nick was cutting up fruit. Youth nights were the highlight of her week … except for the nights when she was rostered on for youth café. She much preferred being out in the hall, playing with and talking to the young people. "I'm not avoiding it. I just don't like it. Besides, I had my nails done this afternoon."

Nick looked as though he was rolling his eyes as the knife sliced effortlessly through the apples he was cutting up. "Wouldn't fixing your car be a higher priority than having your nails done every month?"

"Probably, 'Dad'." Hope pushed herself off the counter and joined Nick at the island bench to help, but Nick grabbed for the apple she reached for.

"Are you sure about this? I mean, you might get some apple under your nails." He made a mock shocked face and Hope tilted her head.

"Very funny. Give me the apple."

the swing doors burst open, and a ruckus from the hall spilled into the small kitchen. Samuel stood just inside the doorway, his brown eyes wide, like a rabbit in a car's headlights.

"What is it, Samuel?" Nick placed the knife down and straightened, his energy perceptibly changing.

"There's a strange guy here." Samuel pointed out in the hall. "He just burst in."

Hope peered out the door. The disturbance had reduced to a dull roar and teens wearing worried expressions faced the hall entrance. Nick was around the bench and out the door before Hope could put a thought together. Samuel followed him out. Only when the doors knocked closed did she spring back into gear.

Hope rounded the bench with hurried steps, and pushed through the doors back into the hall as if she was entering a library.

Trent and Nick were talking to a disheveled young-looking man, while a number of youths stood alongside them. The rest of the group stood afar off, some sharing giggles, some whispering, and others frozen to the spot. Hope turned to take in the guest who had brought youth night to a halt. Tattered jeans, a smudge of some kind—sauce?—over the front of his shirt, and a hole in the side of a green zip-up hoodie that appeared several sizes too large. His bare feet looked dusty with dirty and overgrown toenails. Hope shuddered. Part of her wanted to go over to him, but another part was thankful Nick and Trent were handling the situation.

The man turned, and Nick walked him out while Trent shepherded the curious teens back to rejoin the main group. Hope watched from the kitchen doorway as Dave took to the stage and gestured for everyone's attention. Lexi caught Hope's eye and motioned for her to come over and join the group.

"How is everyone?" Dave looked over the gathered teens. Hope watched their reactions with interest. She was unnerved and could only imagine what the young people were feeling.

As Dave talked, Nick appeared beside her. "You alright there, Meyer? It was all a set-up, remember? That guy, he's a mate of mine from high school."

Hope leant towards Nick, while trying to listen to the feedback the young people were giving Dave.

"What? No way."

"We talked about it at the leadership team meeting, remember?" Nick gave her a curious look. "That was only five days ago. Or were you more distracted by Dylan coming back that night?"

Heat flamed into Hope's face as she looked at Nick. "What?" She spoke through her teeth, while the conversations around them dissolved like the foam on a cheap cappuccino.

Nick side-eyed her before turning back to watch Dave. "Did you think I didn't notice you developed a little thing for Dylan? I'm a cop. It's part of my training to read people."

Hope turned away as if to listen to Dave, drew in a deep breath and blew it out through her nose. The last thing she needed was Nick goading her when she couldn't figure things out for herself at the moment. "What has that got to do with tonight?"

The youths were beginning to relax and she heard a few not-so-nervous giggles as Dave continued.

"Tonight is the practical application of the 'do you love your neighbor' theme we talked about at the leadership meeting. Any minute, Dave will call us into small groups to discuss each person's response to the clearly in need person who stumbled in and help them process what happened. If you hadn't been so distracted that night, you'd remember."

"Nick, Hope. You two joining us?"

Hope turned to see Dave motioning to two small groups waiting for them. All of a sudden, she recalled the details of the leadership meeting and what the leaders' roles were. Nick was right. She had tuned out when Dylan entered and declined her offer to sit beside her.

Unsettled by her reaction to the man who had entered their youth group, Hope asked herself why hadn't her heart reached out to him? She hurried after Nick to take the paper Dave was holding out. The paper didn't slide out of Dave's hand as she grabbed it, and she glanced at him to see his focused gaze square on her. "You got this, Hope?"

Hope nodded. How many other people had noticed she'd completely dropped the ball? "Yeah, yeah. I'm alright. I'll go over these questions with the group. No worries."

Dave released the paper and Hope headed to the waiting group. With a deep breath, she read through the questions and fielded answers all while smiling her usual smile. Inside, she was rattled. She was sure she'd have been the type of person who would have run to the person needing help.

So why hadn't she?

FOUR

"So you and Josh are ... on a break?" Claudia held a couple of drinks over her head as she wove through the throngs of people gathered at Gavin's townhouse and out onto the second-story verandah. "What's that mean?"

Hope took the glass Claudia offered her and shrugged. She was still trying to get her head around Josh's words and work out her current relationship status.

"I have no idea, Clauds. I'm in uncharted territory." She took a sip of the icy cool Coke while taking in the view of the fore-shore. A pair of hooded plovers silhouetted by the setting sun glistening over the expanse of water, lazily wove their way to their nesting place for the night. "I can't get over Gavin's place. It's just gorgeous."

"Ladies."

Hope glanced beside her as Scott joined them, resting his forearms over the verandah railing, holding a drink with beads of condensation running down the sides of the glass. "Hey, Scott."

"Where's Maddy?" Claudia looked behind Hope. Hope turned to look for Scott's girlfriend, but the look on Scott's face wasn't promising.

Scott remained silent.

"What happened?" Claudia gasped. "She was so much fun."

"Yeah well, she decided to be so much fun with someone else." Scott's voice was flat as he spoke into his drink before draining the glass. Ice blocks clinked as he replaced the glass on the verandah railing.

"It must be the week for breakups."

Hope nodded at Claudia's comment, then looked at Scott. Though his slumped posture over the railing hadn't altered, there was a glint in his eyes which wasn't there a moment ago.

"You and Josh too?" Scott looked back into his glass as if more drink might magically appear.

The evening breeze picked up, rocking the party lights above them. Hope watched them sway as she recalled the conversation with Josh. "Yeah. No. I mean, I dunno."

"They're on a break."

Hope tore her eyes from the jingling lights to give Claudia a mock glare. The girl shrugged in response and pushed herself off the railing. "I'm going to get a drink."

Scott turned himself to rest his back against the verandah, crunching the ice blocks from his glass. Hope's phone vibrated in her pocket, and she pulled it out. A message from Trent flashed on the screen. Curious, she sipped her drink and opened the message.

'Behave yourself tonight. See you Monday.'

Hope pocketed her phone and smiled. Trent. He did not like parties.

"I'm sorry to hear about Maddy." Hope finished her drink and crunched on one of the ice blocks.

"Yeah. Me too."

A cheer from inside spilled out onto the verandah as the music level increased and lights flashed inside. Hope side-eyed Scott, a lopsided grin forming on her mouth as he looked back at her with the same expression. "Sounds like Gav's broken out Just Dance on his Xbox again."

Scott held his empty glass up, and Hope tapped his glass with hers. "Let's do this."

Hope and Scott reentered the party, and a roar erupted followed by a challenge for them to step up and defend their previous title. Open mouthed, Hope stared at the score board. Team Tanzi and Elise, two girls from the sports department of House and Home, held the top spot. Hope took a quick glance around the extensive living area and encountered the girls' gloating expressions. Hope mock-glared back at them before holding her hands above her head and strutted towards the cleared area before the giant 80-inch TV screen.

A cheer filled the room, and she laughed as the adrenaline began pumping. Scott appeared next to her, remote control in hand. He rolled his shoulders out then glanced at her before selecting a song for them to dance to from the list.

Just as "Rock Your Body" by Justin Timberlake was selected, Gavin appeared and took the remote off Scott. "Let's make this a little harder for you two. I'll pick your song this time."

The party din raised to a new level as people called out song suggestions. Hope laughed, turning in a slow circle listening to the suggestions.

Gavin began laughing. "I've got the perfect one right here."

The noise in the room dropped notably as everyone watched the selection bar stop at "Buttons" by The Pussycat Dolls. Hope bent at the waist in laughter, silencing the word of caution that shot through her mind. Scott petitioned for a different song. A chant rose to deafening pitch.

"Dance. Dance. Dance. Dance. Dance."

The music started and Scott turned with a shrug. *Sorry* he mouthed, before facing the TV screen. With a drop of her head to compose her laughter, Hope looked back at the TV, game face on. They'd win their title of Just Dance Champs back with this one.

* * * *

"Don't you think you newly singles could have let the dust settle a bit?"

Hands on hips, Hope and Scott stood in Gavin's kitchen watching the next dance team step up to try and beat their new top score. Scott chugged down another licorice-looking drink while Hope caught her breath. She glanced at Claudia as she came alongside her. "What? I'm not single ..."

Gavin appeared at the counter and poured himself another drink. Hope couldn't miss the smirk that tipped Gavin's mouth as he looked between herself and Scott. "That was a good song for you two."

A frown crossed Hope's brow and she missed Scott's reply as "Telephone" by Lady Gaga and Beyonce blared through the open living space. Choosing to ignore whatever Gavin was driving at, Hope leaned into Claudia while pouring herself a glass of icy water. "Sorry. What were you saying?

"You and Scott. I've seen you guys at socials before, but just then? That was a step up."

"Pfft." Hope downed her drink it in one slug. Refreshed, and heart rhythm returning to normal, she replaced the glass on the bench. "He's a work buddy. No more than any other day."

"If you say so." Claudia sipped her drink. "There's a reason why Gavin picked that song. It's not just me who thinks it."

Piqued, Hope turned away from Claudia and watched the latest dance team try to beat the high score she got with Scott. No chance. They had blown the score right out, and it would take a lot to beat them this time. Sure, they had brought it to the room, but they were just following the dancers on the screen. Hope chuckled to herself remembering Scott's moves when a thought of caution ran through her mind at what Claudia had said.

"What are you implying?" Hope asked.

"That, that right there, could be part of the reason why you're *almost* newly single."

FIVE

ope crept into Dave's library and took a seat, Dave was talking about the upcoming Friday night youth night.

"Welcome, Hope. Good to see you." Dave said just as she wriggled into her seat.

Hope glanced around the room. "Sorry I'm late, guys. My car is still at the mechanics—they're struggling to get parts for the old girl—and I missed the last bus for the night, so Liam gave me a lift." While she hated being late, the car ride with Liam had given opportunity to talk to him about her faith, which had to be a good thing.

Nick frowned. "Liam? The tall guy you work with who shaves his head?"

"Yep, that's him." Hope bobbed her head. "I was ringing Mum to get a lift, when he called out to me and asked if I needed a ride."

"What about Josh?" Dylan's tone was careful as he relaxed on the church pew, watching her.

Hope sensed Nick and Dylan didn't like Liam. They always seemed to bristle when he was mentioned, and she didn't know why. Maybe it was the Subaru WRX he drove?

"Why would I ring Josh to come and get me when a work colleague was happy to drop me off?"

Nick cleared his throat but didn't say anything. Dylan continued to look at her for a moment before he turned his attention back to Dave.

"I'm sure it doesn't matter how Hope got here," Lexi said. "The important thing is, she's here."

"Thanks, Lexi." Hope tipped her chin and flashed a smile around the room.

"Dave, how was the overall feeling after last week?" Dylan set his phone on his knee, ready to take notes. "Had any more feedback? I can say some of my small group were not happy to have that sprung upon them."

Lexi chuckled, hugging her notepad against her chest. "I remember a youth activity sprung on me not that long ago. It was confronting, but it was a turning point for me—showed me strengths I didn't know I had, and revealed the thoughts that went through my mind when imagining similar scenarios weren't even close. Really eye-opening."

Dave sat back in his chair, a grin tipping the corner of his mouth. "Well, life is unexpected. Nobody knows what is coming. We need to be rooted in Christ;, our characters need to reflect His, no matter what comes at us. These activities may draw out a response we didn't expect, but that becomes a prayer point for us. Now, as we predicted, there were mixed feelings at last weeks' meeting. Overall, the feeling I get from talking with the youths is that they appreciated being confronted with a situation which revealed an honest reaction."

Hope doodled on her notepad while listening. Honest reaction? So her honest reaction was to be repulsed by people in need? Great. Hope felt herself inwardly recoil at Dave's words. What did her reaction say about her?

"First Thessalonians 3:12." Trent spoke into the silence that followed and Hope looked over at him.

"That's positive to hear," Dylan said, as if Trent didn't speak. "What do we do with that? Do the youth want to be challenged more, or do we continue with how we've been going so far?"

Trent gave her a slight nod, then turned back to the conversation floating around the room. Hope scrawled the text Trent quoted on her notepaper so she could look it up when she got home. With another glance at Trent, she tuned back into the conversation. It was odd everyone kept talking without acknowledging what Trent said.

"What about we introduce a suggestions box?" Nick said. "That way everyone gets the chance to have a say about what we do or teach, but they can also keep their anonymity if they want?"

Lexi nodded. "It would be fantastic to get their suggestions. When should we start?"

"Why not straight away?" Nick sat forward on the pew. "We'll have a box set up around the café this week and announce it at the beginning of Youth night."

Dave clapped his hands and chuckled. "I agree. I'll get a suggestions box sorted this week. Now, back to tonight's business. I'm noticing a trend with some of our regulars, and I'd like to nip it in the bud—or try to, at least. For our icebreaker this week, I thought we could play the Telephone game. It's a simple way to show the misleading and damaging effects of gossip."

"Is that the game some people call 'Whispers?'" Lexi asked.

"That's the one. We line the young people up and give the first in the line a Bible verse to whisper to the person next to them. That person whispers it to the person next to them, and so on until we get to the end of the line, then the final person says the verse out loud. The text will invariably be warped, and that's the message."

Hope nodded. "I've heard of this game. I reckon I know who you referring to."

"Do you have a text in mind, Dave?" Dylan asked.

Dave opened his Bible, flicked through the pages, and read, "Where no wood is, the fire goes out. So, where there is no gossiper, conflict stops. Proverbs 26:20."

After the room voted unanimously on the icebreaker, Dave assigned the leaders their roles for the night, then called the meeting to a close. Hope packed up her bag and filed outside to regroup with her friends around their cars.

"Should we kick on at the Beachside?" Nick leaned against the hood of his car. "Then we can fill Hope in on what she missed."

"Ooh, yes. I'd love that. I haven't had tea yet, and I'm starving!" Hope plunged her hands into her jacket pockets and wiggled into its warmth against the cool night air.

Dylan handed Lexi a helmet and gloves, and then pulled on his own helmet. Lexi poised the helmet in her hands. "I was thinking maybe we should go to a different place for our catch-ups." She pulled on the helmet. Her voice muffled when she continued. "Just to make sure we're not sending the wrong message to any young people who might be out and about and see us hanging out at The Beachside."

"Agreed." Trent slid into his ute. "Just say where."

"Mariners." Dylan flicked his visor down and kicked his motorbike into gear. The roar of the polished Harley Davidson stifled any further conversation. Hope watched as Dylan rode out of the driveway, her best mate tucked in behind him, with Trent close behind. She looked over at Nick as he opened the passenger door on his Clubsport for her.

"I guess we're going to the Mariners then. Jump in."

SIX

The Mariners Inn was quieter than the Beachside Hotel. It was popular with young families, and with the town's clubs and services groups. While Hope was disappointed at the change of venue, she loved the option of balcony dining.

As Hope rounded the top of the stairs with Nick, she caught sight of Dylan and Lexi looking from their table out over the balcony to the moonlit ocean, and something twinged inside her. Dylan draped an arm around Lexi in a tender and protective way and whispered something against her hair. Hope swallowed past the uncomfortable tightness in her chest.

"Hey, guys," Hope slid into a seat opposite Dylan and Lexi, keeping her voice light while forcing her mind to block thoughts of missing Josh. "Where's Trent?"

"Downstairs, ordering you some food," Dylan said as Nick settled into the seat in front of them. He gestured between Dylan and Lexi, a smugness lighting his features. "It's great to see you two looking so comfortable around each other again."

Hope forgot about her hunger and watched the silent exchange between Dylan and Nick. Lexi giggled into her iced tea, a blush spreading over her cheeks.

"How's it going?" Nick winked as he dug his hand into the bowl of peanuts on the table. Dylan's mouth hitched into a lop-sided grin, but he didn't say anything. Lexi was gazing at Dylan, doe-eyed. Hope's stomach tightened and she looked out over the ocean.

"Pretty good so far." Lexi's voice was like a purr before the light smack of a kiss finished the conversation. Grateful she didn't see what she just heard, Hope turned back to her friends and smiled through her disquiet. "I am so happy for you guys. It's been a long time coming."

"Amen to that." Trent reappeared and took a seat opposite Hope, placing a bowl of wedges on the table before her.

Nick leaned across the aisle to pick at the wedges. "Sounds like everyone's a little loved up out at the Saunders residence."

Hope slapped at Nick's hand. "Git outta my food, you. I'm starving. What's happening at the Saunders?"

"C'mon. Just one!" Nick made another reach for the bowl.

With an exaggerated eye roll, Hope offered the bowl to Nick. "Fine. One. But next time we're out, you should order your own. What's going on at Dylan's place?"

"Dylan's boss from the Condors asked Dylan if he could date his mum," Lexi filled Hope in.

Nick took more than one wedge, shoving it in his mouth before Hope could say anything. Hope gapped at him a moment before she huffed and pulled the bowl far away from him. "I said one."

"Meyer, why are you in a bad mood?" Nick spoke through his mouthful. "It's not like you had to prepare the food."

The fine hairs on the back of Hope's neck prickled. Just the sight of Lexi and Dylan all cozied up reminded her of what she didn't have anymore—or did she? This "break" was like having a block of chocolate but not allowed to eat it. And now, sounded like Dylan's mum had something beginning. She sighed and reached for the sauce bottle.

"I'm not in a bad mood. I'm hangry. Now, Dylan, what's going on with your mum?" Hope replaced the sauce bottle, and selected a wedge.

"Are you sure that's all it is, Hope?" Trent asked, laying his fingertips to the back of her hand, and she looked up at him. His light touch stilled her racing thoughts and brought one glaring reality to mind. She didn't want to talk about what happened with Josh, because to voice it sounded like a failure. However, she didn't want to pretend either. Besides, Dylan probably already knew.

Withdrawing her hand, Hope slumped back into the stiff old wooden chair. "Josh sort of kinda broke up with me. He said I need to find out what I want and all that. I don't get it, because what I want is him. So I'm confused. I don't know what to do."

Silence settled over the group. Muffled road noise below and night birds calling floated on the breeze. Hope traced a fingernail along the edge of the wooden table, then let out a long sigh and reached for the bowl of wedges again.

"Well, maybe we can help you in some way?" Lexi's voice was full of positivity.

Hope smiled a whimsical smile across the table at her best friend. "Any help would be appreciated. I'm out of ideas."

Lexi's eyes softened as she looked back at her. "God will help you. Ask Him."

SEVEN

*I*t was late by the time Nick dropped Hope at home. After he'd driven off, Hope stood in the quiet of the night and looked around at the blackened silhouettes of the neighboring houses, up to the twinkling stars above. Everything was peaceful and still, except her thoughts. Nick had filled her in about Dylan's mum on the drive home. Hope was happy for Jenny. She'd been through a lot and deserved to be happy. So why did it bum her out?

Hope made her way slowly down the winding path towards the recessed entrance to her family home. The sidelights were aglow, signaling someone was up. As she drew closer, muffled voices rose in competition with each other. Hope stalled on the doorstep, hand on the handle. Her parents were arguing again. She closed her eyes and breathed deeply of the brown boronia scrubs that lined the path behind her and debated her options.

Did she go in and go to bed or, go in and try to suggest that her parents get help and stop arguing all the time?

Hope's jaw clenched. She'd go in and go to bed. Maybe she'd look at moving out.

Hope clicked the handle, opened the door, and slipped inside. She closed it whisper-quiet behind her, and crept into the loungeroom and across to the stairs leading up to the bedrooms.

Ryan's door was closed, so she continued past to her room.

With a grunt Hope, launched herself towards her bed and landed on her stomach. Making herself comfortable, she dragged her bag over and pulled out her phone to send Lexi a message.

Hey, Lex, random question. Ever think of moving out?

Just texting the words sent a quiver of excitement through her stomach. Imagine that. Moving out. Starting afresh. Hope flipped herself over, tucked an arm behind her head and stared at the ceiling for a moment. Would Lexi be up to moving out with her if she made the move?

Hope's phone beeped.

I have, actually. Moreso since Shaun started making moves to leave. But I wouldn't leave before I finish uni. Should be all finished by end of July though … almost finished my last unit. Yay! Why?

Hope beamed a smile. Only another two months and Lexi would be finished her Bachelor of Youth Work. Seemed like yesterday when Lexi had signed up for the flexible delivery six-year part-time course, and it looked like she would finish in five. Hope couldn't be prouder of her. She hit reply.

Well done! Seems like only yesterday you started.

Hope held the phone to her chest and looked up at the ceiling again. She was happy for Lexi, but her achievement just reminded Hope of her lack of achievement. What did she want to do? While she was thankful to have a job, the confines of the role were starting to chafe. She wanted a challenge, to see more people, experience more things ... but what could she do to tick all those boxes?

Dear God, please don't let me spend another year of my life working at House and Home. Surely you have something more for me?

Hope sighed and switched on her TV. Then, after signing up for a job search app, she scrolled the listings. Nothing grabbed her interest or matched the criteria she'd filled out. Was she being too particular?

With a frustrated growl, Hope placed the phone on her bedside table and turned her attention back to the TV. A few clicks later, she was checking the latest Netflix recommendations. Finding one that appealed to her, she nestled back against her pillows and tucked her arms behind her head. Until something better happened in her life, she'd just have to live vicariously through a good rom-com.

* * * *

Hope tossed and turned during the night, her mind filled with future ideas and plans from short term to long term. The thought that kept her awake was what did she want to do for a career? Her mind played over idea after idea, but she couldn't see herself committing to anything for the long-term.

Sleep refused to give her mind ease, so Hope rose early and decided to walk to work.

With a strut worthy of the catwalk, Hope strode into the Bridgeshore Plaza and made her way through to House and Home. As she headed through the store towards the staff room, Scott came out the doors in front of her. "Morning, pussycat."

Scott grinned as he moved towards her, his pace not slowing. "Don't remind me."

As they passed each other, Hope turned and walked backwards. "I still can't believe you danced like that."

"It's called taking one for the team." Scott held up a fist as he kept walking

Chuckling, Hope continued through the staff room doors to her locker. That night would be a hard one to forget. She frowned as she reached her locker as a thought flashed through her mind … what Gavin had said about the song choice he picked for her and Scott. What Claudia had said about others thinking the same things. Had Scott said something about her? Hope shook her head and drew in a deep breath. She opened her locker, put her bags inside, and checked her reflection in the mirror before closing the metal door with a clang. She would not get caught up in workplace drama and gossip. She just wanted to have fun and live God's purpose for her life.

As soon as she could find out what that was.

Today was a new day, and she was going to take Robs advice for once and leave her personal life at the door. She finally had her car back, basketball was on tonight, it was her turn to score with Lexi on the roster which meant a fun night was coming up.

EIGHT

"Arguing over the coffee?"

Lexi's voice held a note of disbelief. Hope glanced at her, nodded, and turned back to watch the game.

"Are things getting that bad between your folks?" Lexi murmured, just before the deafening half-time siren wailed over The Valley basketball stadium. Hope gave a nod as she tapped the last score into the electronic scoring box, then picked up a pen to scrawl down the figures on the scorecard. Truth was, she'd been getting used to her parents arguing. Now it was more annoying how they could switch it off as soon as someone else appeared.

It was clear Lexi was worried—everything from the look in her eyes to the way she turned her body to face Hope. Nothing else mattered to Lexi right now. Hope sighed, regret weighing her stomach down. They were like sisters, telling each other everything.

"I didn't want to rain on your parade with Dylan."

"Hope." Lexi's tone revealed her disappointment. "That's ridiculous. You ok?"

Hope glanced away. She wasn't sure. She wanted direction in life, a reliable car, parents who got along, and a man to stand beside her even when she was a hot mess. She chewed one of her nails as she thought.

"Hey, girls. How's the card looking?"

Hope snapped her head up as Shaun's voice lightened her mood. Though she saw the grin on Lexi's face in her peripheral vision at the question of how she was being left unanswered. Hope sat forward on the hard bench seat and grinned at Shaun. "Good. You boys are on fire tonight."

Shaun turned the score card towards him just as another teammate jogged up to check the card. Lexi poked Hope under the table, and she looked over at her.

What? Hope mouthed.

Don't what me. Lexi mouthed back as the boys discussed the card.

Hope giggled, drawing the boys' attention to her. She quickly composed herself. "By the way, sensational foul on number forty-seven over there, Shauno." Hope pointed the butt of her pencil across the court to a young man holding an ice pack to his forehead. Shaun looked over the court to his opponent then back at Hope, his expression impish.

"If you were watching the game, you wouldn't have seen that."

Hope lifted a shoulder. "Yeah, well, maybe I wasn't watching the game ..."

The siren blared again. and Shaun's mouth tipped just before he turned and jogged back to his team. Hope felt the warmth in her cheeks as she looked back at the scoresheet.

"Are you done?"

Hope glanced at Lexi. The girl's expression made Hope grin all the wider. "What?"

"Oh, don't 'what' me. You two are the biggest flirts I've ever met." Lexi wagged a finger in Hope's face. "Shaun is still with Renee, I might add."

The stadium erupted as the opposing team scored a goal from outside the wing. "I'm not flirting. It's just a bit of fun." Hope kept her eyes on the game. "We're not hurting anyone." Lexi finished updating the score. "That's debatable."

Hope swallowed past the rising irritation in her throat. Lexi's disappointment radiated in her mind like Josh's words.

"The problem is you're openly flirting with a man who's in a relationship, and you're a youth group leader. Do you remember what the Bible says about stumbling blocks?"

A referee blew his whistle, and an argument broke out between the referee and the player he'd called the foul against. A second referee joined them and called a time-out.

Hope stopped the clock. She knew, but didn't think that applied to her. She hid her irritation behind an appreciative smile and laid a hand on her best friend's leg. "I'll be good, I promise. I guess that's just the way Shaun and I have always been with each other."

Lexi's eyes narrowed, and her steely grin told Hope she wasn't convinced. Lexi turned her attention back to the game. "Do you think your folks would get counselling?"

Hope kept her eyes on the game and tried to ignore the weight in her heart. She had considered asking them, but even imaging that conversation felt odd, let alone trying to have the conversation.

Anyway, they were scoring a basketball game. This block of time was reserved for lighthearted banter and how's-the-weather conversations.

"Hope?"

Hoped blinked and looked at Lexi. "Yeah?"

"You need to mark that three-point score in for the Rangers, and the foul number four made against one of our guys." Lexi pointed to the areas of the scorecard Hope needed to fill in.

As Hope marked in the missed parts of play, she was aware Lexi was watching her. When the final siren rang out, the players shook hands, then headed to their respective benches for sweat towels and water bottles.

Lexi shuffled out from behind the score box. "Come for a wander outside and tell me what's on your mind."

The night air held a chill, and Hope turned up the collar of her emerald-green merino wool coat as she and Lexi walked out of the basketball stadium. Once they'd reached a quiet part of the busy car park, Hope plunged her hands deep in the coat's pockets and turned to Lexi. Lexi's blue eyes focused hard on her, and Hope smiled a resigned smile.

"What's on my mind? Lots of things. Stuff Josh said. Things I'm hearing at work about me and a colleague. My parents' issues. My car. And why aren't I getting any answers when I keep asking God for direction?" Hope wriggled further into her coat and looked down at her suede ankle boots as a breeze swirled around the lamplit car park.

"Wow." Lexi's breath came out as a puff of smoke. "That's a lot on your plate. I'm always amazed at how you keep smiling."

"They say it takes more muscles to frown than to smile." Hope scuffed her boot along the gravel carpark and looked up at Lexi's soft giggle. "I don't like being in a grump. Things get me down like everyone else, but I tend to bounce back pretty quick."

"That's true. That's one of the reasons we love you so much." Lexi embraced Hope, and a lump formed in Hope's throat.

"Can I help you with anything?" Lexi released her and gave her arm a rub.

"I could use some extra prayers." Hope sighed. "I don't want to stay working at the plaza, but I don't know what Jesus wants me to do. And I want to understand what Josh's problem is with me. I've hurt him, but don't know how. It kills me."

Lexi hummed in thought. "Of course, I'll keep you in my prayers. We all know you'd never intentionally hurt anyone. Maybe he's just giving you some space … or giving himself some space?"

Hope looked back at her and shrugged. "Who knows?"

"What's this thing at work you mentioned? Rumors about a colleague?"

Hope gave a dismissive wave of her hand. "I'm sure it's nothing. But I don't want drama at work. Though, you know that impending feeling when you feel something is going to happen?"

Lexi chuckled, nodding her head. "Yes, I do."

"I have that in the back of my mind, too."

A siren rang out from the stadium. Hope looked over to see people spilling out from the entrance milling around those trying to get in. Ryan's game would be coming up soon, and she was always front and center for it. With a head gesture back to the stadium, Hope turned to make her way back inside, and Lexi followed her lead.

"Just remember," Lexi's voice was hushed as they made their way across the now-quiet car park. "The more you search for Jesus, the more you'll blink on the enemy's radar." Hope unhooked a piece of hair the wind blew into her lip balm and gave a slow nod of her head.

That was just another worry to tuck away in the back of her mind.

NINE

ope stared at her reflection in her dressing table mirror, then back at the makeup influencer she was following on YouTube. Taking close note of the way the colors were blended around the woman's eyes, Hope dug into her makeup drawer and fished out the new shimmery plum color she'd bought. After a subtle dust across her eyelids and another brush of mascara, Hope examined herself again. Her green eyes were popping now, just like the woman she was watching. Perfect.

Five minutes later, dressed in a pair of skinny jeans and white turtleneck top, with a red jacket draped over her arm, Hope grabbed a pair of mid-calf tan boots and skipped from her room. Youth night was starting in ten. If she had a good run, she'd be on time this week.

* * * *

The hall doors banged shut behind her, and she dumped her coat and bag on the kitchen servery counter before trotting towards the stage where her friends and Dave sat. "Sorry I'm late."

"It's all good, Hope," Dave said. "There isn't much setup for tonight and we've got the icebreaker sorted, so we were just chatting."

Hope jumped into a bean bag and tossed her hair. "Great! Catch me up. How's everyone's week been?" As soon as the words left Hope's mouth the hall doors opened with a crash and the first of the night's youth entered. Hope smiled brightly over her shoulder at them, watching them interact and laugh.

"Hey, before I forget, Shaun's having a housewarming party tomorrow night starting at eight." Lexi kneeled beside her on the carpeted stage floor. "It's kind of a last-minute open invitation. Are you free? I thought it might take your mind off things."

"Let me check my calendar." Hope laughed brightly. "Of course I'll be there. Give me details."

Lexi stood and drew Hope up with her. "Great! I can't imagine a night more boring than hanging out with my brother's friends without you."

Hope grinned as they made their way backstage to get the props for the icebreaker games. She felt the same about her brother's friends. "Are the boys invited too?"

"Yep." Lexi shouldered a giant net bag of balls. "Shaun said it's open. Even invited his new neighbors. He's had a huge week with moving house, and he just wants to kick back and relax."

"Well, we can certainly help him do that." Hope lay half a dozen Hula-Hoops over her shoulder and picked up an indoor cricket set. "Until then, let's go show these kids how to play ball."

The hall was packed with what must have been one of their bigger turnouts as she went about her role for the evening, setting up the game stations, introducing herself to new faces, and sharing jokes with regulars.

"Hey, Hope." Nick appeared and spun a basketball on the tip of his finger. "Up for a game?" Hope eyed the half-dozen youths behind him. "Sure. Is this leaders against youth, or boys against girls?"

"Boys against girls!" The teens shouted almost in unison.

Hope laughed as she snatched the ball off Nick's fingertip. "Boys against girls it is. Let's go."

Nick and Hope faced each other, one of the youths threw a ball up, and the game was on.

Four players a side on a half court was manageable, but they soon had the attention of most of the room. More players appeared on the teams behind the play, and it was soon five a side with subs, and the rest of the hall was opened up to a full court.

"Two minutes left," Dave called before too long.

Hope called for a time-out, catching her breath as she locked arms in her team huddle. She was well and truly ready for the end-of-night café break. She could already smell the food and drinks Lexi and Dylan organizing.

"Ok, girls. We're one point down, and there's only two minutes on the clock. Here's my plan. Stacey, I'll knock it to you. Nat, you run for the right wing while Kate heads for the right corner. Tam, you hang around the top of the key, ready to run in. Stacey, pass to Nat, then you make for the left corner. Nat pass to Kate, Kate pass it back to me as I run in. I'll pass it to you, Tam, then Tam fire it straight back to me and I'll finish this off with an inside hand layup."

Heads bobbed up and down.

"Reckon you can pull that off?" Stacey asked. Hope peered over their huddle to see Nick talking to his team. "Yeah. My brother and I practice all kinds of shots. I think I'll nail it."

"Let's go, girls!" Nick's clapping echoed around the hall. "Time-out over."

Confident of victory, Hope broke the huddle and crossed the floor to the center where Nick was waiting.

The noise from the boundary lines had increased. Even Lexi and Dylan were leaning out the kitchen servery window, and Trent stood ready to umpire. Hope narrowed her eyes on Nick while watching Dave in her periphery. The moment the ball left Nick's hand, she launched herself after it. A fingernail must have won the tap. Hope landed mid-turn to see if her plan was playing out.

It was.

Hope sprinted to her position to receive the ball from Kate. Hope dodged the oncoming attack, smoothly passed to Tam, then darted through the key to wait for the pass back from Tam. It came as planned. Hope grabbed the ball mid turn and started her planned run up, faking to the right before moving the ball to her left hand ready to leap for the net.

Her boot suddenly dug into the hall floor, and she tumbled to the ground. The ball turned over and Hope accepted the help of a teammate to get back on her feet. Hands on hips, Hope waited for the ball to be thrown in. As she sprinted down the hall, following the play, an air horn blared.

Game over.

The boys won by one.

Raucous cheers filled the hall as the boys began jumping all over each other and teasing the girls over their loss. Hope called the girls together, congratulated them on their efforts, and made her way over to the café for a much-needed drink.

She slumped into one of the chairs and blew her breath out. That was embarrassing.

"Tough break there, girl." Nick's voice broke into her thoughts. "I thought you had us there for a sec."

Hope shook her head. "I'm shattered. Can't believe I tripped over my shoe!"

Nick clucked his tongue as he tapped her shoulder and took a seat at the table with her. "Let it go. It was just a game—"

"Nice play there, Hope. I see what you were trying to pull off."

Hope sat up and pivoted on her chair at the sound of that voice. Shaun. Laughter bubbled out of her, and she was surprised by the glow that spread throughout her body at his appearance. "Oh hello! Is it two years ago?"

Shaun grinned as he pulled a chair out, placed his keys and phone on the table, and lowered himself into the plastic café-style seat. "Has it been that long?

"Yep. Scary how fast time goes." Hope's mind flashed back to the last time Shaun attended youth group. He'd been her first crush, and seeing him at youth had been the highlight of every week. When he left, it felt like her world had dulled a little.

"Where'd you learn to play like that?" Shaun interrupted her thoughts.

"Ryan and I practice all kinds of shots together."

"You should join the Vikings. The ladies' teams need a few extra numbers."

"I don't think I would play competitively. I just help Ry practice." Hope knew she was rushing her words, but Shaun's appearance was so unexpected, it had thrown her. However, she hadn't missed the compliment. He thought she was a good basketball player. She beamed a smile at him as Nick coughed.

"So what brings you here?" Hope kept her eyes on Shaun and kicked Nick under the table.

"I was unloading a box of old sport equipment when I realized I don't use it or need it anymore, so I thought I'd donate it to the church," Shaun said, "I did think about giving it to Lexi tomorrow night, but I needed an unpacking break."

"How is the move going?" Trent asked.

Hope half-listened to the boy's conversation. Her thoughts turned inward, marveling at how her crush on Shaun had just faded away. He was still as dreamy as ever, all the more so now he'd grown a stubble beard to complement his textured hair. But her heart was with Josh now. Looking down, Hope picked at her nails and wondered what Josh was up to and if he was thinking about her at all.

"You all coming tomorrow night?"

Hope registered the question and looked up just as Trent was declining the invitation. When Shaun's hazel eyes turned to her, she nodded.

"I wouldn't miss it."

TEN

"Hope speaking" Hope sang into her phone while perusing her wardrobe for something to wear to Shaun's party tonight.

"Hey, girlfriend. It's Bec!" the friendly voice said. "How are you?"

Hope gasped and stopped riffling through her clothing. "Bec? How am I? How are you? Where have you been?"

Bec Welson, Hope's counterpart around the Valley Tigers Football club, was one of the most fun people Hope had ever met. When they went out, didn't matter what they did or where they went, fun was always on the cards.

"Are you still with Zac?" Hope was so happy to hear from Bec, who had recently returned from a trip overseas. "Did you get a new phone? I didn't recognize the number."

"I am and yes, I did. Lost mine somewhere in the Rhine." Bec said airily. "But I heard about you and Josh. What is the go with a break? Is that a breakup?"

Hopes smile fell away. "I have no idea."

Bec hummed into the receiver. "Are you two on friendly terms, at least?"

"I guess so." Hope resumed flipping through her clothing. "Although we haven't spoken to each other since the night he called it." Finding the top she wanted, she flung it over to her bed, then began searching for coordinating pants.

"Would you feel comfortable coming to a club function, even though you two aren't together? You can still hang out with us girls."

The idea ignited within Hope. She had loved the club functions. The dressing up, the dancing, the food, the fun and occasional innocent flirting with the other players. She lifted a shoulder in thought. "Sure. Can't see why not. I miss hanging out with you, and I can't wait to hear about your trip."

Hope held the phone out from her ear at Bec's cry of excitement and laughed. "You must have missed me too."

"Mark your diary, woman." Bec was getting down to business. "Next Saturday night at the club rooms. Seven o'clock start, food and drinks provided, and the theme is seventies."

Hope laughed again, envisaging the skintight sunburst mini-dress, with oversized white collar and front zip detail her grandmother had given her. "Oh, I know exactly what I'm going to wear already. What are you going to wear?"

Bec's tone turned cheeky. "Oh, something short and plunging, with lots of sequins."

"You'll look amazing!" Hope grinned. Saturday night was going to be a blast, but first there was a housewarming party to get to. "I better run, but I'll see you on Saturday night"

"See you Saturday, sweets. Be good." Bec sang before hanging up.

With a flick of her wrist, Hope sent her phone from her towards the bed where her bag waited and scooped up the new perfume she'd bought. She spritzed the perfume into the air, breathing in of its deep musky floral notes as she twirled in the mist. Her excitement about the house party was knotting her stomach and energizing her spirit.

With a final twirl in front of her mirror and confident nod of her head at her outfit, Hope grabbed her bag and phone, then skipped out her room and out the front door to head over to Shaun's new place.

* * * *

With a slam of the front door, Hope stomped back into the house and tossed her bag over to the couch. Of course her car would let her down.

"Hope? Honey?" Mrs. Meyer put down her magazine. "What's wrong?"

Hope gave a long growl as she snatched up her bag from the couch and fished out her phone. "My car is what's wrong. Everyone else I know has a reliable vehicle. Why can't I?" In a few moments Hope had Lexi's number up, and pressed call.

"Oh, honey. I'm sorry. You'll have to look at buying another car." Mrs. Meyer rose and crossed the plush pile carpet towards Hope. "You're spending more money keeping that yellow beast on the road than repayments on a loan would cost."

Hope nodded as Lexi answered. She held Mum's arm. "Just one sec, Mum. Hey Lex, are you at your bro's?"

"Yeah, got here about ten minutes ago. The place is jumping. Where are you?"

"My car won't start. Dad's away, and Ryan is out—like I should be. Could you come get me?"

"Oh sorry, we came on Dylan's Harley."

"Is Nick there?"

"Yeah, but with Alice. I can ask him for you if—"

"No. No. Don't worry about it." Hope dropped her head into her hand and shook her head. It was pointless. She couldn't afford a taxi and it was too far to walk. "You guys have a great night. Have a dance for me, and I'll see you Monday night."

"I'm sorry your plans haven't worked out, sweetie. Can I make you a drink?" Mrs. Meyer asked. Hope released her mum's arm. A heaviness formed in her gut and she toyed with her phone, unsure of what she wanted. With a heavy sigh she looked back at Mum. "No thanks, Mum. Think I'll just have a long bath and go to bed with a book."

Fifteen minutes later, Hope sighed as she slid down into a bath full of jasmine-scented bubbles, watching the flames flicker from her soy candles.

This was not how she saw her night playing out.

The cheery message tone from her phone broke her absent-minded stare and she reached for the phone, hoping it might be Lexi offering to pick her up.

Just after nine on a Saturday night, and Hope Meyer is on messenger?'

A lopsided grin formed on Hope's mouth as she read Scott's message. She hit reply.

'I should be at a housewarming party, but my car wouldn't start. So I'm having a bubble bath and a date with a book instead. What are you doing?'

Hope blew some bubbles off the back of her hand while she waited for Scott's reply. She could see he was typing. Then not typing. Then typing. She chuckled. What was he deleting?

'Trying to study but got distracted by the little green dot beside your name.'

He was right. She wouldn't normally be on Facebook on a Saturday night, because she'd be out in the moment. Having fun. Noticing Scott was writing something, she chewed a nail and watched the screen.

'Now I'm distracted by the mention of a bubble bath ... LOL.'

Hope rolled her eyes, a retort forming in the back of her mind when she saw he was typing again so she jumped in first.

'Whatever unit you're trying to study must be riveting...'

'Heard from Josh? Are you two still on a break?'

'LOL. Agricultural economics and not really.'

Though she sensed he was fishing, it didn't bother her. Everyone around her was coupled up and had careers and reliable vehicles, so she enjoyed the ego boost. But Josh had said he still considered them together. So if she was to go down this path with Scott, she'd have to break up with Josh, and she didn't want to do that. She sighed.

"God help me. What is going on?"

'I'm not really sure what my relationship status is, TBH.'

Again, she could see he was typing a message, then wasn't, then was again. Hope looked up at her flickering candles. Maybe she should message Josh.

But say what?

A beep brought her attention back to the screen.

'If he ever lets you go, just know you won't have far to fall. Better get back to it. Night.'

ELEVEN

"ine. Mine!" Hope grabbed for the morning paper as soon as Dad rose and dropped it back onto the breakfast table, snatching it from her brother. She sunk back into her chair, smiling a smug smile over the paper at Ryan, who rolled his eyes before he rose from the table, taking his breakfast plates with him.

"Why don't you check your job search app and let me see the weekend sport results?"

"I already checked it. Just curious to see what the paper has listed. You can have the paper in a few minutes."

Ryan moved from the kitchen and disappeared down the hall. "Nar. I'm going out to my bike. Catchya."

Hope flipped each page, past news articles and ads, looking for the employment pages. As she turned over each page, her leg bounced, quickening with each page. As much as she wanted a new job, the whole concept freaked her out. She wanted her next move to be a lifelong career move.

Only a small amount of pressure.

"Hope?"

"Yeah, Mum?" Hope called back, keeping her eyes on the paper. The employment pages had a fair bit on them this morning that was different from her app.

"I'm taking your brother to the dirt bike track. Don't forget the dog."

Hope waved a hand over her head. "No, I won't. Bye."

A moment later Hope heard a quiet conversation sprinkled with laughter float down the hallway. Surprised, she looked towards the doorway, straining to make out what her parents' murmuring voices were saying.

They sounded … happy. It'd been a long time since she'd heard her parents share a laugh together. Barking interrupted her gentle reverie. Ivory, the family dog. Hope stood with a start. With a flip of her hand, she closed the paper and hurried outside to get her dog before Mum reminded her again.

Hope slipped on her sunnies, looped the lead on Ivory and headed for the beach.

The day was overcast and the air held a cold bite to it that offered a number of reasons to abandon the daily run in favor of a good book, or a rom-com movie marathon under a fluffy blanket at home. However, she zipped her sports jacket up over her white racerback top and purple, pink, and white marbled three-quarter length leggings, set her fitness tracker, and began jogging before she reached the beach. Ivory, a white mixed breed Labrador cross she adopted from the local pound, needed no encouragement.

Ivory set a steady canter pace beside Hope and she smiled, listening to the thump thump thump of her runners on the bitumen road. The beach was in sight, a murky blue-grey expanse that blended almost seamlessly into the gloomy canopy above.

It wasn't forecast to rain, but based on the sky, Hope wasn't sure she was going to believe the weather channel. She set an alarm on her watch, then reached a hand down and unlatched the lead from Ivory's collar. "Only a quick run today, girl. Let's go." Hope broke into a sprint as her dog galloped away from her so fast that her feet barely touched the ground.

The beach was empty, and a lazy haze hung, restricting visibility, but Hope could see her dog's white coat running in the shallows. Hope kept her pace steady, breathing in the cold salty breeze and controlling her exhale, keeping her eyes on her dog.

All of a sudden, Ivory turned back and ran towards her. Hope squinted at a shadow that had materialized out of the haze in front of her. She kept her pace as Ivory came alongside her, uninterested in whoever may be sharing the beach with her this morning, When Ivory stopped, Hope pulled up and looked back at her dog.

"What's up, girl?"

The dog looked uneasy, looking back the way they'd come, then trotting toward Hope and sitting in front of her. As Hope knelt to check the dog's paws, a deep rumbling growl emanated from within Ivory's chest. At the same time Hope felt the hairs on the back of her neck stand on end. She looked up.

The figure stood far enough off that she couldn't make out details aside from the fact they wore sunglasses and a heavy black coat with a hood. Ivory growled again. Hope stood and kept her tone light. "What a day for a run on the beach aye?"

Silence followed her question. The ocean continued to roar beside them, and Hope toyed with Ivory's lead. Should she clip it back on, or keep it in case she needed it for self-defense? She cleared her throat. "Can I help you with something? Are you lost?"

The figure looked out over the ocean then back at her. "You're friends with Dylan Saunders, aren't you?" The voice was male and sounded middle-aged.

A warning zipped up Hope's spine. She knew the question was rhetorical. "Why?"

Ivory growled again and took a step towards the figure, as he looked to step back.

"Tell him someone is looking for him."

A wind whipped around Hope as the figure turned and walked away. Ivory nosed her hand. She looked down at the dog and took the warning. A shiver rattled its way up Hope's body and she shook out her arms before clipping Ivory's lead on.

"C'mon girl, let's get outta here. I gotta talk to Dylan!"

TWELVE

reathless, Hope burst through the front door, unclipped Ivory and dived for the loungeroom coffee table where she'd left her phone. She found Dylan's number and hit call, still shaking from her encounter on the beach.

The phone rang and rang and rang. Hope drummed her fingernails on the coffee table while waiting for him to pick up, her mind a flurry of—she hoped—irrational thoughts. Where was the strange guy now? Would he come back? Did he follow her home?

"Hey, Hope. How's it going?"

Hope gripped her phone and started pacing. "Dylan. I. Just got home. I was running. At the beach. Someone—"

"Hope, slow down. What's going on?" Dylan's concerned voice cut in. "Are you ok?"

Hope took a long breath in and blew it out as she moved to the loungeroom windows. Her heart was about to bust out of her ribs. She peered outside through the lace window coverings.

"Hope? What's wrong?"

She turned and sat on the plush pile carpet, startled by the sharpness in Dylan's tone. "Sorry. Sorry, I'm fine. Just spooked, I guess."

"Tell me what's happened? Start at the beginning."

Hope took a deep breath and tried to focus on telling Dylan what happened. "I went for a run on the beach. The beach was empty, but this dude appeared from nowhere and set Ivory off. She was sitting in front of me, growling at him. He asked me if I was a friend of yours, and when I asked why, he told me to tell you …" Hope took a long breath.

"Tell me what?"

Hearing the words in her mind sent a fresh shudder travelling through her body. "He told me to tell you, someone is looking for you."

The hairs on her arms stood on end and she looked over her shoulder out the window again. She heard Dylan sigh. "Yeah. I've heard. Trent told me a couple nights ago."

She frowned. "What do they want?"

"It's to do with Jack. It's about money, we're sure."

Hope gasped and covered her mouth. "So can the police sort this out, or are they going to … you know, visit you?"

A humorless chuckle came down the line and Hope gripped her phone harder. "Oh my, they already have?"

"Yeah. Couple of months back. While I was playing. Look, Hope, I want to talk to you guys about this, but I've gotta run. You're ok, so don't go jumping at shadows. Alright?"

Hope laughed a little too loudly. "Why would I be jumping at shadows?"

"I've known you long enough. Just, be cool, ok?"

Hope felt her shoulders relax a little and she nodded. She was worried about her friend—and herself, to be honest—but Dylan knew about what was happening and still sounded relaxed. He'd have his finger on the pulse. Plus, from what she'd heard about Lachlan, the man knew a thing or two about how to navigate the mess Jack had got himself into.

"Ok. I'll chill out. Sorry to call you in hysterics. I sprinted home and couldn't catch my breath."

Dylan's warm chuckle came down the line. "All good, Hope. See you at leadership tomorrow night. Talk more then."

* * * *

Hope knew she was only bodily at work when she meandered herself towards the storeroom, Rob's note in hand. A shoulder brushed by her arm, and she jumped at the touch as Claudia hurried by.

"Whoa, girl. Who's on eggshells this morning!" Claudia laughed as she hurried past Hope on her way out the back. Hope plastered a smile on her face and upped her pace toward the storeroom. She couldn't concentrate. Dylan told her she was ok, and she probably was. After all, it wasn't her they were looking for. Hope rubbed her arms as she walked.

She had to stop thinking about things—Josh. What to do in life. And now, some lurker on the beach. At leadership tonight, she could talk to Dylan and Nick. Maybe then her brain would stop overworking in that department at least.

Hope came alongside her colleague and looked at the note from Rob: an order form to check off received goods. Not a task in her job description.

"I'm not on eggshells. It's just my mind is a million other places."

Claudia laughed again, making notes on the paper in front of her. "Really? Cos that's unusual."

Hope sniffed. "Yeah, yeah, righto." Hope placed the invoice of goods form on the workbench. "Ok, so tell me this. Why does Rob want me to do Scott's job out here?"

Claudia looked over the form, then back at hers. "I've got something similar to do. Maybe Scott's away. I haven't seen him this morning."

"Okay, but it's crazy for Rob to ask us both to be back here. I'll head back out on the floor while you're here and see if Liam has any jobs for me."

The morning dragged on. Hardly any customers came by, and Hope's areas were dusted, faced, and replenished. Even the music piping over the sound system seemed to be quieter. Struggling with lack of motivation, Hope meandered over to the makeup area and remembered the weekend coming—the dress-up night at the Tigers clubrooms.

The dark cloud hovering in her mind drifted away almost instantly. The smells of perfumes, colors of lipsticks and eye shadow shades filled her mind with fantasies of the weekend and energized her spirit.

Josh would be there. She hadn't heard from him since he ended things. Hope picked up a red shade of lipstick as the book she'd just finished flashed through her mind. The lead won her man back by playing off the affections others had towards her, but that wouldn't work for Hope. The more other people showed interest, the more Josh backed off.

A deep frown crinkled her forehead and she put the lipstick back. Everything seemed upside down.

God, I don't understand. I'll grant Josh the Dylan thing. I know, I spaced out a bit there in fantasy, but the other things Josh said? I'm just out having fun. I love people. Lord, you know this. I love helping people and making them laugh. Does Josh want me to stop having fun or something? Help me to see where his insecurities lie.

THIRTEEN

Hope half-listened to Dave's welcome. The leaders were all in his office, and while she knew Dave did a welcome and devotional every week before they focused on the task at hand, this evening she wished they'd address the elephant in the room first.

Hope looked at Dylan across the room. He appeared relaxed as he sat next to Nick, phone on knee ready to take notes as usual. Was he going to bring up the creep on the beach looking for him, or would she? As if sensing her gaze, Dylan's gaze shifted to hers a moment before he returned his focus to Dave.

"Hope, what are your thoughts?"

Hope raised her eyebrows with a sheepish smile. "Ah, sorry, Dave. What was the last bit you said?"

"Excuse me, Dave." Dylan sat forward on the pew. "Can I jump in for a moment?"

Dave sat back in his chair and made a sweeping gesture around the room.

"Guys, there's something I need to let you all know." Dylan's eyes grazed Hope's as he looked around the room, and her heart geared up a notch in readiness to hear what was going on. She sat forward on her seat and rested her chin on her hands.

"As you all know, my brother Jack got himself mixed up with the wrong kind of people, which all came to a head recently. However, what I hadn't told any of you except Nick was that we had some shady people visit our home one afternoon while I was playing. Mum says they asked all kinds of questions, wanting to know where Jack was."

"I kept this between Nick and myself. I figured the less everyone knew, the better. I'm sure you've all seen enough news and movies about the drug industry to guess what happened. They couldn't find Jack, so they approached the people closest to him. And it seems they're continuing to do so, even though Jack is now in custody."

Dylan looked at her, and Hope straightened. "Hope."

All eyes suddenly turned to her and the tension in the room rose. Was she meant to pick up the story?

"What's going on?" Lexi's words broke the uncomfortable air that had settled over the room and Hope turned to her, hearing the tremor in her voice. She glanced around the room, nailing Dylan with a questioning glare. He cleared his throat.

"Hope and Trent have both had visits from people wanting to find someone—Jack, we assume. We don't know what they're after, but we wanted you all to be aware."

Nick blew his breath out before resting his elbows on the church pew behind him. Trent sat unmoved, eyes scanning the room, while Lexi looked like she was struggling to put her thoughts into words.

"Dylan, this is, serious!" she managed to get out as her hands toyed with the notebook on her lap. "Hope, what happened? Are you ok?"

Hope blinked. Hearing Dylan tell the story made it more real. What would happen next? "Yeah, I'm ok, Lex. Just spooked."

"What happened?" Lexi pressed.

"A guy baled me up on the beach yesterday when I was out for my morning run. He kinda came out of the fog hanging over the beach. He told me to let Dylan know someone was looking for him."

Lexi shook her head before turning her eyes downward. Hope looked around the room. Seemed everyone was in reflection. Hope lowered her eyes too. Lexi was right. This was serious. She'd never considered that whatever Jack had got himself into could affect her one day. She looked up at Dylan to ask him a question but found his gaze locked on Lexi.

Dave cleared his throat. His hands were linked over the papers scattered over his desk and he appeared deep in thought. "We better keep Dylan's family and those closest to him uplifted in prayers for protection until this is all sorted out."

"I should have told you guys what was happening months ago, but a part of me just wanted to ignore what was happening." Dylan rubbed his forehead. "Stupid and naive of me, I know."

"Hindsight is a wonderful thing." A look of empathy crossed Dave's features.

Nick rapped Dylan on the back a few times. "C'mon mate, it's all getting worked out. Things take time. But let me assure you, we've got the best of the best on this case."

Hope crossed her arms while listening to the conversation. It was a comfort knowing Nick was a police officer, and, in her close circle of friends. She just hoped he was safe too. Surely those after Jack would also know Nick was a connection of Dylan's too.

FOURTEEN

Hope pulled up outside the Tigers clubrooms, turned off her car, and sat for a moment. Memories flooded her mind of when she came here hoping to catch Josh's eye, of when they used to walk in arm in arm.

Would he be happy to see her tonight? Should she give him a hello hug? The corner of her mouth tugged down to one side as she looked towards the clubhouse. She was never usually unsure.

The seventies music was thumping, and the number of cars in the parking lot suggested it'd be packed inside. Tossing her indecisions over her shoulder, she took one last check of her reflection in the rearview mirror. She'd go in and be herself. Whatever happened, happened.

Hope tucked her clutch under her arm and slid out from the car. She had gone to a lot of trouble to ensure she made an entrance tonight—had her hair colored and shaped into a flicked-up bob, nails done, a light spray tan, and she wore an expensive perfume she knew was Josh's favorite. Not to mention the trouble she went to finding affordable white over-the-knee boots in time. She was here to have fun!

The clubrooms had been transformed into a disco, complete with a color tile dance floor with built-in lights. There was even a bubble machine blowing from somewhere in the room, and a mirror ball hanging from the ceiling. Hope looked around the room taking it all in, when a hip bump almost knocked her over.

"Hey, girlfriend!" Bec squealed from beside her.

Hope squealed in return before wrapping Bec in a bear hug. "It's so good to see you!"

Bec stepped back and looked Hope over. "You look … hottt!" She mock fanned her face. "Josh is gonna die. That's the perfect revenge dress."

Hope felt a tightening in her stomach. She didn't want revenge. Before she could explain, Bec had her by the hand, and they were headed to the bustling dance floor.

Though she danced with abandon and shared laughs with everyone around her, Hope found herself searching for Josh in among all the people. Had he seen her already?

Bec leaned in after a break in the DJ's set. "Hey, I better go check in with Zac. Wanna come?"

Hope shook her head and made a drinking gesture with her hand. "I'm going to go get a drink."

Hope rested against the bar and scanned the room, unable to relax until she'd seen Josh. It was hard to identify anyone at a dress-up disco—there was nothing but a sea of big hair and overly patterned costumes mingling under the flashing lights. A finger tapped her on the shoulder, and she turned back to the bar.

"What will it be, miss?" The barman barked.

"Water only for her," a voice shouted from behind her. Hope looked over her shoulder.

Max.

Grinning, Hope rolled her eyes and looked back at the barman. "I'll have a Coke please, no ice."

When the barman went to get her order, Hope turned around again to face Max. He smirked at her. "Coke. You know that's a stimulant?"

Hope couldn't help but grin back. His eyes were saying something completely different as he looked her over. Hope rested her elbows on the bar behind her. "I do. Thanks."

"It's been rather quiet at these gatherings without you." Max moved closer to speak over the music though his eyes never left hers. "And dull, without that smile lighting the room."

"Coke, no ice." The barman's gruff voice shouted from behind her.

Hope went to turn around, but Max quickly handed a note over her shoulder to the barman. "It's on me." He collected her drink and handed it to her.

"So who are you dressed up as?" Hope took the glass off him, purposefully ignoring his comment, and eyed his white suit and open-buttoned black silk shirt.

Max slipped an arm around the curve of her back, guiding her away from the bar through the milling people. "I'm John Travolta from *Saturday Night Fever*."

Hope eyed him sideways. "But can you move like him?"

"You know I can." Max winked and turned his collar up before strutting out onto the dance floor. Impressed, Hope took a sip of her drink while she waited for what he was about to do, when he turned, struck the iconic seventies pose, then began doing the lawn mower.

Hope choked on her drink and held a hand up to her mouth as others around began laughing and egging him on. He moved seamlessly into the sprinkler, playing back to those watching. Hope burst out laughing as he moved towards her, gesturing for her to join him.

Unable to resist his offer, Hope leaned towards the closest table to put her drink down.

"Hope!"

Hope's laughter caught in her throat. She knew that voice, even over clanging seventies music. She turned. All trepidation at seeing Josh again vanished at seeing his kind face smiling back at her.

"Wow." Josh breathed against Hope's hair as he embraced her. His freshly shaven cheek against hers, the sensation of his breath upon her skin, and his lingering hug speared her heart. She closed her eyes. She'd missed the feeling of being wrapped in his arms. He pulled back and held her at arm's length, looking over her a moment before his hands dropped away. His gaze was full of adoration, and a warmth lit Hope's entire body. She missed him so much.

"Thanks." Hope lifted a shoulder, unsure what to say next.

Josh leaned in. "What did you say? I can't hear you over this noise."

Hope allowed herself to smile at him, then lay a hand on his arm, stepped into him and spoke against his ear. "I said, thanks!"

Josh held a hand out to her. "Wanna head outside? Easier to talk out there."

Hope nodded and placed her hand in his, allowing Josh to lead her outside.

The night air was freezing, and Hope rubbed her arms as she looked up at the clear sky. Not a breath of wind rustled the canopy trees, and the stars glittered like diamonds tossed onto a black velvet matting.

A jacket came around her shoulders and she closed her eyes. She loved Josh's aftershave. The warmth of it always made her feel like Christmas morning—happy, content, with a sense of excitement.

"Thanks." Hope opened her eyes to see him come to stand in front of her. "You look good too, by the way." She looked over his attempt at seventies dress up—a half-unbuttoned hot pink shirt, white flared pants, and pair of oversize star-shaped sunglasses now pushed up on top of his head.

Josh chuckled as he pocketed his hands. "It's all I could come up with. How long did you spend getting ready for tonight?"

"Oh, about a week" Hope grinned as Josh looked her over again. He rubbed the back of his neck. "That dress is ... incredible."

Hope looked over herself then back at him. "It's seventies, isn't it?"

"Ah, yeah."

An awkward silence fell over them and she knew Josh wasn't sure where to look. Something moved inside her as she studied him. Surprised to realize that he was uncomfortable, she rubbed her arms through his jacket and looked away, unsure what to say.

"Gotta tell ya, it surprised me. Never seen you wear anything like that before."

A giggle bubbled out of Hope as his gaze swept over her again, and she shimmied her shoulders at him. "You like?"

"Ah." Josh chuckled, crossing his arms. "I do. What I didn't like was what people were saying about you."

Hope's smile fell away. "What were they saying? Were they talking about my dress? It's a dress-up party. Everyone's dressed up. What's wrong with my dress?"

"Nothing. You've fulfilled the brief and more—"

"So what's the problem?"

Josh looked away and sighed a lengthy, frustrated sigh. Hope fixed her glare upon him, ready for when he looked back at her. Tonight was supposed to be a great night, so why were they having an argument in the cold carpark?

Josh's expression was firm when he turned back to her. "The problem is what you say and what your actions say, Hope. They don't add up. We've discussed this before."

"And what do I say that my actions don't say? Apart from tonight. Talk in general terms."

"Ok. Take earlier on. I noticed you the moment you walked in. I saw how you moved on the dance floor and how you danced." Josh gestured to the clubrooms. "I saw you at the bar with Max, the look in your eyes, and that grin you get on your mouth when you're being cheeky or suggesting something …"

Hope shook her head. "So I'm not allowed to have fun? I'm not allowed to share jokes with people or—"

"This is what I'm talking about Hope. It's double standards."

This was unbelievable. Hope turned away, her arms falling to her sides with a slap. She shrugged out of his jacket, turned, and held it out for him. "Well, maybe we should break up good and proper. It's so obvious that I'm apparently not good enough for you."

Josh took the jacket. "That's ridiculous—"

"I am who I am, Josh. If you can't handle that? Well, that's not my problem."

Hope turned and strode towards the clubroom's side entrance. Anger bubbled through her veins, and her breathing came short and fast. She reached the door just as Josh reappeared beside her.

"Hope, please, just—"

"You know something, Josh?" Hope grasped the door handle. "Maybe it's you who needs to get their head sorted out."

With more effort than needed, Hope yanked the door open and strode inside. The night was shot. All she wanted to do now was go home and forget about everything.

Including Josh.

FIFTEEN

Hope turned off the shower and stepped out into the steam-filled bathroom. After wrapping herself in a pink fluffy bathrobe, she wiped the steam off the mirror and looked back at her reflection. Her lackluster eyes were still rimmed and darkened from eye makeup that wouldn't budge, and the freckles over the bridge of her nose were now visible against her pale skin. Hair wet and hanging limp beside her face made her look drawn and older than her twenty-three years.

Welcome to single life.

With a long sigh Hope turned away from the mirror and set to making herself presentable.

Half an hour later, Hope plodded down the stairs in a pair of distressed skinny jeans and a white t-shirt, just to catch Dad give Mum a quick kiss as he headed out.

Mum headed back to the kitchen and Hope followed, a question burning on her tongue. Mum looked back as they walked. "You're up late. Good night last night?"

Hope lifted a shoulder. "It was ok. Where's Ry?"

"He's outside fixing his bike." Mum headed for the coffee machine. "Want a cuppa?"

"Where did Dad go?" Hope took a seat at the table and gave Mum a nod to the drink offer.

"He had to go into the office."

Hope grabbed an apple out of the fruit bowl and crunched a bite before pulling out her phone to check her job search apps. She couldn't focus. When was the last time she'd seen Dad give Mum a kiss? She looked up as Mum approached with the coffee. "So ... you guys aren't arguing as much lately. What's changed?"

Hope took the mug Mum handed her and watched closely as Mum seated herself at the table. She made a study of the mug in her hands for a moment before looking at Hope.

"Well, one night after an argument, I went for a shower and I was pouring my heart out to God about all the things I saw were wrong with your Dad, when a verse flashed into my mind."

Mum took a sip of her drink. When she replaced the mug she turned back to Hope, her countenance full of peace, her voice soft. "How can you say to your brother, 'Let me take the speck out of your eye', when all the time there this a plank in your own eye?"

Hope sat back in her seat. She knew that verse but had never heard it applied in a manner she understood. Mum placed a hand on her leg.

"Sweetie, I took this as a gentle reminder from God that I have just as many flaws as your Dad. So I asked God to help me and show me where my faults lay. I tell you, I noticed the difference fairly quickly."

Hope took another bite out of her apple as Mum sipped her coffee again. Recognizing parts of herself in what Mum had said,

Hope chewed her mouthful and sent an earnest prayer heavenward for God to do the same for her.

"Ry and I noticed the difference too. We're just happy to know you and Dad are getting along better. It was embarrassing to hear you guys arguing all the time."

Mrs. Meyer dropped her head and toyed with the mug in her hands. "I know, sweetie. We are all a work in progress. The world gets to us sometimes, and warps how we see things. But when we come to God, He helps us see things clearly. Remember He is the God of relationships. If something isn't working, He'll help you understand why."

Hope's phone beeped beside her. Before she considered looking at it, Mum exhaled loudly and rose from her seat. "You answer that, darling. I have housework to do."

Taking another bite out of her apple, Hope drew her phone to her and opened the message.

'Hey, Hope. What's on for today? Wanna hit the beachside market? Lexi.'

Hope felt a slight smile creep along her mouth. Nothing better to clear her head than to meander around the beachside market with her bestie. She hit reply.

'Love to! Meet you in the car park in halfa. X'

* * * *

An hour later, Hope strolled alongside Lexi throughout the stallholders of the local market, burrito for breakfast in hand.

The morning was bright, the air fresh and filled with the sound of demanding seagulls and the crash of the surf. Hope breathed deeply of the market smells as she checked out the items for sale under the multicolored buntings and flags. The organic food, the homemade candles, merino wool slippers, clothing, donuts...

"Oh, doughnuts!"

Hope doubled back at Lexi's giggle. Hope threw Lexi a helpless look, before taking her place in the queue. Surely doughnuts could follow burritos. Besides, everyone knew her weakness for sweets. Lexi gestured towards a plant stall, and Hope lifted her hand in acknowledgement.

Armed with the bag of hot jam doughnuts, Hope crossed over the dusty path to catch up with Lexi. She was looking over a shelf full of garden gnomes. Hope licked the cinnamon sugar off her fingers. "Something for Dylan's mum?"

"Well, her birthday is coming up, and she seems to be quite taken with this gnome village she's built." Lexi picked up a gnome in a car and looked it over. "I don't think she has one like this though."

While Lexi bought the gnome and had it gift wrapped, Hope looked over the gathering crowds. A young couple grabbed her attention as they laughed together at a nearby hat stall.

Josh came to mind. Hope had brought him here for their second date, and they'd played around with the different hats at that same hat stall. She blew her breath out, popped the last mouthful of doughnut in her mouth, then dusted off her hands.

"Whatchya thinking about?" Lexi appeared beside her, fitting the wrapped garden ornament into her bag. "You look far away there."

Hope tore her gaze off the happy couple and offered a smile at Lexi. "Oh. Had a heavy chat with Mum this morning. Still processing, I guess. I need a cuppa."

Lexi gestured towards a cappuccino vendor. "Well, how'd last night go? Start there."

Hope considered how she would answer as they waited in line. Lexi would be expecting a highly animated retelling filled with detail and inflection. She shook out her hair and huffed. "Well, it started great, then ended ... with my relationship status confirmed as single."

Lexi gasped but didn't say anything. In the silence that followed, Hope imagined her best friend trying to form some sort of encouragement to offer.

The line moved quickly, and it wasn't long before Hope had her steaming hot cappuccino in hand, and she took a seat at a nearby bench seat. Hope slurped the foam off her drink and watched Lexi with interest.

Lexi looked like a movie character on pause. Frozen, mouth open, her drink untouched. Despite the circumstances, Hope found a chuckle bubble out of her. "Hey. I'm the one that's newly single. You still have your man."

Lexi blinked and drew in a long breath. "Oh wow. I'm so sorry. I'm just shocked, I think. What happened?"

Hope took a sip of her drink. "Oh, we got into another argument about the same types of stuff."

Lexi smiled gently as she brushed her fringe aside. "I don't know what to say. I mean, Dylan's told me how crazy Josh is about you. Maybe he's just worried about getting in too deep with you if you're going to leave him for someone else?"

"But I don't want to leave him. I ..." Hope clamped her mouth shut. The words *love him* dissolved over her tongue but burned into her mind. Did she love him? She swallowed hard, the market noises faded away leaving only the echo of her thoughts in her mind.

"Maybe he's looking for some sort of change in you? You know, actions speak louder than words."

Hope felt a sudden lump in her throat. What Lexi said rung so close to what he'd said to her when he called the break. *If it's me you want, show me.*

Out of nowhere, a defensiveness rose up within her. She sat back into the bench seat and crossed her legs. "I don't know what to do, but I'm not changing myself for a guy. Looks like I don't need to worry about that now. I'm free as a bird. There are other options out there who'll take me as I am." Hope took a sip of her drink, her thoughts flittering over to land on Scott.

Lexi raised an eyebrow. "I didn't say to change yourself for a guy. You change to better yourself or to challenge yourself. Take House and Home. You not satisfied working there, so what else do you want to do?"

"Ha. That's the million-dollar question. The million-dollar question."

Lexi finished off her drink, then snapped her fingers and pointed at Hope. "Ok then. What about … This is just a suggestion."

Hope sat forward on the bench seat and angled herself towards Lexi, pushing thoughts about Scott to the side while she focused in on her friend. A heaviness formed in her gut. She was not good with constructive criticism, and that's what was coming. "Ok, hit me with it."

Lexi smiled. "Well, what about trying to be on time to things from now on? Or early? Taking control of what seems like little things can make a huge difference with how you feel about yourself and how others see you."

Hope tested the idea. While it felt hard hearing it, she had to admit timeliness was something she had to work on. She knew it. She was disorganized. Always had been. But easy enough to turn around if she put her mind to it.

"Alright. I'll wear that. In fact, I'll be early to Dave's tomorrow." Hope pointed back at Lexi to emphasize her statement.

Lexi drew her cup up as if to toast what Hope had just said. "I'll pray for you. Be prepared for the struggles that will come when you try to make positive changes."

Hope lifted her drink and toasted with Lexi. Her stomach fluttered with the idea of what lay ahead for her.

"Guess I'll jump those hurdles when they come."

SIXTEEN

*H*ope whipped the strap of her bag around her neck, and skipped out the front door, pulling it shut behind her. She was going to be on time to leadership tonight, and it felt great.

Hope parked out the front of Dave's almost fifteen minutes early. She flicked on the interior light of her car and opened up the Kindle app on her phone. A few clicks later she had the latest *recommended for you* book up and reclined her seat to get the first chapter in before the meeting started.

All too soon, the sound of Dylan's motorbike drawing near broke into her alternate reality. Hope put the phone away. With a victorious grin, she climbed out of her car as Dylan pulled his bike up next to her and shut off the engine. Lexi chuckled from behind the helmet and Hope lifted the visor for her friend. "Look at me. Early!"

Arms outstretched, Hope waited for Lexi to climb off the bike and hug her. Even though it was day one, she could get used to this.

Dave's smile was as warm as ever as he welcomed everyone into the library, though Hope didn't miss his fleeting look of surprise at seeing her enter the library first. Unable to wipe the grin off her face, Hope took her seat and turned her attention to Dave.

"Welcome, everyone." Dave opened the meeting. "Tonight I wanted to get straight into business. Let's crack open our recently implemented suggestions box, and see what our young people would like to do."

Murmurs of agreement echoed around the room. Dave gestured to Lexi to take a few slips out of the box sitting on the coffee table. Lexi rose, selected three slips of paper, and handed them to Dave. He opened the papers, then laid them out on the coffee table for all to see and discuss.

Hope tilted her head to read the papers:

Angels and demons discussion.

Soup kitchen outreach.

Special item for church—choir?

"Soup kitchen?" Hope looked around the others. Lexi and Trent looked enthusiastic while Dylan and Nick mirrored her own expression. "Is that like where we make soup and buns for people?"

Dave leaned back in his chair. "In a roundabout way. Yes. A soup kitchen is a hospitality-based outreach aimed at those who may be homeless or less fortunate in our communities. Seems at least one of our young people out there has a heart for grass-roots ministries. Ok, leaders, any thoughts on the other two suggestions?"

Nick turned to Trent, "You're with the worship team. Would that one about the choir be something you could lead?"

Trent gave a slow nod of his head as he looked to consider the option. Then, leaning forward he looked square at Dave. "I like the Angels and Demons suggestion. We should do a focus on that some night. All young people need to understand those dynamics that play out around them every day."

Goosebumps ran up Hope's arms at Trent's focused look. She continued to stare at him, unable to look away, while conversation continued on around her. Why did that topic resonate with him so much?

"Personally, I like the soup kitchen idea." Lexi's voice broke into her thoughts, and Hope forced her mind to focus back in on the room. "We could contact a homeless shelter in the city, and ask if they need volunteers on a Friday evening. It'd be good for the teens to see that side of life."

"I have a contact in that area of ministry." Trent sat back in his seat, linking his hands behind his head. "I'll touch base with them and get some things organized for us."

"Can I get in on that with you?" Lexi asked. Trent nodded, and Lexi made a note on her notepad.

Hope felt like she was watching a tennis match.

"I guess we're going with the soup kitchen thing, then?" Nick's droll tone dropped into the conversation to no one in particular, and Hope grinned across the room at him.

Dylan chuckled. "It appears so, man. Hey, how about having some Bibles available at the soup kitchen, in case someone wants one?"

"How about a prayer request box, too?" Lexi's head was still down, scribbling across the page. Hope craned her neck a little to see what she was writing.

Dave gave a clap of his hands. "I think the soup kitchen idea has grown legs and is now running, Nick. Yes, let's work towards this suggestion, and Trent, I hear you. I've noted down that we'll do an angels and demons theme night soon. But first, let's remember that the soup kitchen type of outreach drives home importance of our witness. It's what's on display. Is what we say reflected in what we do? Is what we believe reflected in how we act? Sometimes we are the only Bible others will read."

"That's something I think about a lot." Lexi looked up from her notepad. "I have relived many conversations and moments in my head, wishing I could have done things better."

Nick cleared his throat. "Second that."

"That's why we need grace." Trent's voice came from the back of the room. "Grace teaches us how to live in a way that lifts up Jesus. It's not an excuse to continue living an unchanged life."

Hope swallowed the lump that formed in her throat. For some strange reason, she felt Trent had spoken just to her. Things Josh, Lexi, and others had said to her came back to mind and she grimaced.

Grace teaches us how to live...

Teaches us...

Suddenly she wasn't sure if she knew how to live. She'd lost Josh over how she lived, but what was wrong with her lifestyle?

God help me understand this. I need your grace.

Confused, Hope let her gaze travel over the room when her eyes fell upon Dylan. Why did she start crushing on him? Because that seemed to be the start of everything going pear-shaped. Sure, he was good-looking, but she didn't want him. She knew that much. She wanted Josh.

Maybe it was what Dylan represented?

She wanted to be fought over? Fought for? Rescued?

Hope frowned as her brain fired ideas at her. Where did these ideas and desires come from? Looking back at Dave, she tried to concentrate on the plan for youth night coming up, but her thoughts wandered to what Mum had said. She'd asked God and He was helping her ... Hope could see that. Her parents were getting along again and even showing affection to each other.

Readjusting herself on the couch, Hope cleared her throat and tried again to focus in on the conversation around her. Dave had rounded his desk and was perched on the corner of it as he brought the meeting to a close. The room was abuzz with an energy as final comments were made and notes taken.

Hope spun her pencil over her fingers while she listened. She'd never had anything to do with homeless people. All she knew was how they were described in books or represented on TV. If the youth night about loving your neighbor was anything to go by, she wouldn't be any good with this task. How would she relate to them?

She moved uncomfortably on her seat as a hard realization dawned on her.

She wasn't sure if she wanted to be a part of this activity.

SEVENTEEN

The old carpeted staircase of the Mariners Inn creaked underfoot as they made their way up to the balcony seating area. Hope's stomach grumbled and she inhaled the delicious smells of roast chicken and thyme floating in the air.

"You know, I am really looking forward to this group ministry idea." Lexi sat in the seat Dylan pulled out for her.

Hope took a seat opposite, and drew in another deep breath of the scents around her. "Why is that?"

"Well, it's one thing to talk to the youth each week about Jesus." Lexi reached for the glass jug on the table and poured herself a drink. "It's another thing entirely to help them be His hands and feet in the community."

Trent picked up the menu, "It'll also help them learn about themselves. Help them identify the gifts God has given them."

"Plus, projects tend to bind people together. They'll come out of this more united as a group," Dylan added.

"Reckon they'll wanna do more outreach after this?" Nick lent back in his seat and toyed with one of the glasses set out on the table.

"It's possible. All it takes is a spark for a fire to start." Trent signaled for the waiter.

Lexi swallowed a mouthful of water and replaced her glass on the table. "Remember when we did the Random Acts of Kindness car rally that ended at Pastor Walker's home at a banquet?"

Hope nodded, "Yeah, that was a really fun night."

"And that the aim of that night was to illustrate how living in a way that reflects Jesus can encourage others to come to the banquet? Well, after that night I made some enquires to an organization called Adventist Volunteers. They're keen to do a presentation to our youth one night about what they do. They do all kinds of mission work, all over the world."

Dylan lent back in his seat and rubbed his jaw. "I remember you mentioning them. What do you think—that we should have this Adventist Volunteers group come in shortly after the soup kitchen night?"

Hope felt her brain start to hurt. They were all so enthusiastic, so why wasn't she?

"Guys, I hate to interrupt. Circling back to the homeless shelter visit, I'm not sure how I feel about the idea. I don't know anything about homeless people or helping them or what even to say to them. All I can base an understanding on is what I've seen in movies or read in books—"

"You and your books."

Hope paused at Nick's muttered comment and frowned at the top of his head while he picked at the peanuts on the table. "What's wrong with books?"

"Nothing is wrong with books."

"So why the dig about me loving to read?"

Nick looked up at her, his gaze as cool as his tone. "There's nothing wrong with books as long as the fantasy a book can create doesn't cross over into reality."

Hope held Nick's stare. Something about what he said seemed to bounce off the walls of her mind. A soft chuckle from Lexi broke the standoff. "Homeless people are just people, honey, and you are fabulous with people. Oh! Maybe Adventist Volunteers is something you could look into?"

Hope ignored Nick and gave Lexi an appreciative smile. "I'm hardly volunteer type material. I mean, I still have no idea what my spiritual gift is. What will I do at this soup kitchen night?"

The waiter appeared. After they'd placed their orders, Hope turned her attention back to Trent. He poured her a drink, then himself.

"I agree with Lexi. You're great with people. In fact, a number of our youth started coming because you invited them."

Voices echoed Trent's compliments and Hope took in their encouraging expressions. That was a gift? It was so natural for her to try to include people and make them feel welcome. "So I just need to be me then?"

Lexi covered her mouth as she giggled. "Of course!"

"Maybe a little quieter." Dylan made a reducing gesture with his thumb and pointer finger as a grin tipped the corner of his mouth. Hope laughed and tossed her napkin at him just as the waiter returned with their orders.

"I know, I know. I'm loud. I like to have fun and laugh a lot."

"You're more than that." Trent sat back as the waiter began to fill the table with plates of food. "Trust God has you right where He wants you."

Lexi lifted her glass, "Hear! hear! That goes for all of us."

After Trent offered a blessing over the food, Hope got stuck into her vegetarian lasagna and chips while listening to the conversation around her. As conversations circled around past and present attendees of youth, Dylan's younger brother flashed into her mind. As soon as a break in conversations allowed, Hope pointed a chip at Dylan.

"By the way, how is Jack doing?"

Dylan replaced his drink and cleared his throat. "We're waiting for the plea hearing date to find out what his sentence is. He's home under summons at the moment and has been the easiest to get along with for a long time."

Lexi nodded her head. "It's true. He even offered to wash my car last time I was over."

"Lachlan is really good with him too. He just seems to know the right things to say to get Jack thinking about things differently." Dylan brushed some crumbs off the tabletop and picked his drink up again. "He can motivate him in ways Mum and I never could. It's like …"

He fell silent as he took a drink, and Hope caught the look Lexi gave him. Nick looked out over the balcony, and Trent leaned across the table and rapped Dylan's arm. "It's ok if having Lachlan around reminds you of your dad. He hasn't been replaced. God has sent what your family needed."

Hope chewed at her thumbnail while the silence hung over them like a wet blanket. She was sure each of them where recalling the moment Dylan told them his Dad had died in that car accident. Sharing that moment together, the intense emotions, had bound them as friends forever.

But Trent—as usual—was right. Lachlan would never replace Dylan's dad, but it was undeniable he was an answered prayer. The support he was giving the family was uplifting to watch. Dylan had battled for years to hold things together, and now he could relax a little. Hope drew a long breath in and straightened in her chair. The mood needed lightening. "Soooo, this is intense."

A droll grin tipped Dylan's mouth. "I know. We all tried to get Jack to come back to youth, but he wasn't interested. It was always going to be hard when he crashed, or Mum met someone. I agree with you, Trent. Lachlan is exactly what we needed."

Dylan blew his breath out and looked at Lexi. "I haven't seen Mum so happy in a long time."

"Me either." Lexi looked back at Dylan. Her smile gave Dylan's words two meanings and Hope dropped her head as her heart began to thump with deep heavy whacks against her ribs.

Ouch.

Single life was hard.

EIGHTEEN

Hope tried to look busy at work, but she knew her lazy dusting of clothing racks and facing stock wouldn't cut it. Afterall, she was already blinking on a disgruntled managers radar, so nothing would be good enough.

"Psst, Hope!"

Hope started at the voice hissing her name and whirled around. Lexi was approaching, a worried look in her widened eyes. Hope hastened to her.

"What's going on?"

Lexi looked to swallow hard as she rapidly shook her head. Hope looked either side of them. Everything was quiet. She leaned towards her. "What's happened?'

"I just had a visit … from someone looking for Dylan." Lexi's voice held a slight shake.

Hope felt the hairs on the back of her neck rise. A shiver ran up her spine and she shook it out. "What did they say?"

"It's not so much what they said." Lexi brushed her fringe aside with a shaky hand. "Just that they know where Jack is, so why visit his friends?"

Hope had seen enough movies to send her imagination into overdrive, but she tried to stay calm. "I'm not sure. But Dylan said we were safe. Have you told him?"

Lexi fiddled with the zip on the bag slung over her shoulder. "No. He's having a meeting with Lachlan and another guy from the club this morning. I messaged him then took my break and came down here to talk to you."

"Ooh, what are they meeting about?" Hope asked, pushing away her worry.

Lexi brightened as she looked from her bag back to Hope. "They wanted to discuss the possibility of him being an educator for a program they run for young people. It focuses on the effects of drugs and alcohol on sport and things like that."

"Oh, wow. That's so Dylan!" Hope whispered through her beaming smile just as her pager buzzed on her hip. She turned to see who was paging.

"Ooh, that's Liam. I better get back to work." Hope smoothed out her skirt. "You all good?"

"I'll be looking over my shoulder when I leave this afternoon. Apart from that, I'm good. You?"

Aware of Liam waiting, Hope tried to think how to summarize a myriad of thoughts. "You know, I know these things are happening, but it doesn't seem real. Like it's something I've read in a book, you know?"

Lexi embraced her. "I know exactly what you mean. We need to keep praying."

Once Lexi had gone, Hope looked around her surroundings and felt an odd sensation crawl along her skin. Lexi was right. Why were these people visiting Dylan's friends when they knew where he was?

Suddenly, feeling vulnerable, Hope turned and hurried out the back.

Not until the storeroom door firmly closed behind her did Hope realize she'd been holding her breath. Dylan had said they were ok, but she wasn't so sure.

When she reached the receiving bay desk, Hope rested an elbow over the work desk and spun the pen over her fingers, looking back from where she had come. A shiver ran up her spine as the cool of the storeroom began to leech through her cotton shirt.

Turning back to the work desk, Hope looked over the paperwork attached to the clipboard in case that was what Liam wanted her to go over. A door closed behind her. Its loud thud echoed throughout the quiet, and Hope spun around with a gasp, dropping her pen.

Liam slowed his stride to a hesitant amble. A mix of confusion and humor crossed his features as he approached. Hope laid a hand over her chest and let out her breath with a laugh.

"You scared me to death!"

"I can see that." Liam came alongside her at the work desk. "Everything ok?"

Hope bent to pick up her pen. Rising, she spun it again over her fingers while trying to speak through the pressure in her chest. "What took you so long?"

A frown crossed Liam's forehead as he pulled another clipboard out from under his arm and put it on the table. "I got held up with a customer."

Hand on hip, Hope stopped her pen spinning and pretended to look over the clipboard. It slipped out from under her eyes, and she looked back at Liam, who'd withdrawn it and held it by his side.

"That clipboard is staff rostering for next month and you're looking at it like you're trying to figure it out. What's going on?"

The storeroom doors banged open again and Hope jumped. Masking her fright with a laugh, she scratched a non-itch on the side of her neck as she tried to work out what to say. Liam's shrewd eyes held hers with an expression, daring her to make something up.

"Am … I interrupting something?"

Hope tore her eyes away to see Scott, who had paused back from where she stood with Liam. She shook her head, grateful for the interruption. After all, how could she tell her manager that she and her friends were potentially being stalked by a drug cartel?

Liam signaled for Scott to join them. "No, Scott. In fact you saved me paging you. Got ten minutes?"

"Sure." Scott looked between Hope and Liam and walked over to them.

Liam pulled out a folded piece of paper from his rear pocket, opened it, and placed it on the work desk. "Can you both go through these items for your departments we've received today. Accounts say the invoices don't add up, and they're trying to finish up end of financial year figures."

Hope nodded. Scott took a step towards the worktable and looked over it. "Sure, no problem."

"Great." Liam headed off. "Page me if you get stuck," he called over his shoulder as he left.

Hope massaged the back of her neck, anticipating the bang of the storeroom closing, and shook her head. When she looked up, she encountered Scott's bemused expression. She raised an eyebrow.

Scott chuckled. "Don't give me that look. Rob bothering you again?"

Hope grinned as she looked away. Scott was intuitive at times. "Not Rob, but yes, something is bothering me. I don't want to talk about it though."

"Can't, or won't?"

"Bit of both." Hope feigned a study of the paperwork Liam had left them, feeling her resolve to not talk about it starting to slip. Scott leaned over the work desk next to her, his shoulder brushed alongside hers. Surprised, she looked over at him and was struck by the concern in his eyes.

"C'mon, fess up. What's going on?"

She'd never seen him so close or so intense. Her eyes travelled over the slightly hardened lines of his tanned face, while the subtle scent of his earthy cologne wove its way into her senses. The memory of their online conversation came back to mind, and heat ran up the back of her neck. Hope blinked. The thought so fleeting sent a slight thrill throughout her.

She dropped her gaze back to the paper Liam had given them. That conversation would wait for another day. There were bigger issues to deal with right now.

"Nothing important. Let's dig into this before Rob tries to roast us?" Hope glanced at Scott. The look on his face told her he wasn't buying her attempt at diversion.

A playful grin tipped the corner of his mouth. "I meant what I said the other night."

Hope matched his grin as she toyed with her earlobe. It would be too easy to jump from Josh to Scott. He was a great guy, from a stable family in the country. Plus they always had a lot of fun together.

But her heart was still with Josh.

Hope gave a nod. "I know you did."

NINETEEN

"So what are we doing for Dylan's birthday tomorrow?"

Hope walked beside Lexi towards the hall for youth, helping carry the items needed for the planned icebreaker. The weather looked to be great, and Hope had her fingers crossed that fun was on the cards. She needed to let her hair down and burn off some steam—they all did.

Between Dylan's brother's issues, Nick adjusting to his role as a first responder in police matters, and her recent breakup, they needed a night to recharge their spirits.

Lexi balanced the box she was carrying on her hip as she opened the hall door. "Volleyball on the beach and dinner somewhere along the foreshore."

"Fish and chips?" Hope passed by Lexi and headed to the stage to set her items down.

"Dylan wants to try something different. So I thought about that new pizzeria that's just opened … Oh, what's it called?"

Just the mention of pizza cramped Hope's stomach and she made a sound of delight. "Oh, I know the one you mean, but can't remember its name. It's got a great alfresco dining area, almost right on the beach."

"That's the one."

"Sounds great." Hope was emptying the items in her box out onto the stage when the hall doors banged open behind them, and she heard the boys enter.

Not twenty minutes later, they had five tables with chairs surrounding each one set out for the planned group activity, and the youth café set up.

While Trent and Nick went to prepare the café food for later that evening, Hope moved around the trestle tables, placing handfuls of the magazines Lexi handed her on them. Lexi then placed containers of glue, sticky tape and scissors on each table, while Dylan followed behind placing a giant piece of carboard on each table.

Dave appeared from the adjoining church office just as they'd finished setting up, and Nick and Trent had rejoined them.

"Ok, everyone, the youth will arrive shortly," Dave said. "Let's gather for a quick prayer before we get started."

Not a moment after Dave had said Amen, the hall door opened again and the first of the evening's youth entered. With a yelp of surprise, Hope excused herself and skipped over to the face she had been looking for, for months: Josh's little sister, Kaitlyn. "Hello! You came!"

Thrilled that the younger girl was equally excited to see her, Hope listened as Kaitlyn explained she had wanted to come for a long time but wasn't sure if she should. Hope dismissed her concerns and set about introducing her to some of the other teens who had arrived while they were chatting. Happy that Kaitlyn had slipped into the group without any awkwardness, Hope excused herself after seeing Dave jog up to the stage.

Joining her friends against the side wall, Hope leaned against the cool terracotta bricks and watched the youths' faces as Dave explained the activity before them: they had fifteen minutes to go through the magazines and find pictures showing what they thought the good life was.

As Hope watched, the young people seated at the tables began cutting out pictures of couples, jewelry, big houses, island vacations, motor homes, caravans, tables laden with food, and sport trophies. While the room was filled with laughter and pictures handed between each other, Hope felt a disquiet creep into her mind. It all seemed to be screaming: this is what success looks like. She had nothing like it, and she'd never have it if she couldn't find a career and make some substantial money,. What did that mean for her?

"Ok time's up," Dave called out. "How do your poster boards look?"

Hope listened as each table gushed about the collages they'd put together, talking about their dreams and aspirations while Dave indulged their animated chatter.

"They all look terrific. Fantastic life plans all of you have. But let me put something to you. Do any of you currently live lives like this, or are you drawn to these images because you've seen them in movies or TV or online, or read them described in books? Why do we want lives like this when the Bible instructs us to live simple lives? I see even some of you had pictures of great banquets of food, though the Bible says to eat simply. We need to be on guard for what is placed in front of our eyes, because by beholding we become changed."

At Dave's signal, Dylan moved from where he was seated and moved around the tables handing each youth the keychain Dave said he was going to organize. Hope looked down. She knew what text was on the keychain. It had sat heavy in the back of her mind since Dave read it out at a leadership meeting.

Incline my heart to Your testimonies, and not to covetousness. Turn my eyes from looking at worthless things, and revive me in Your way. Psalms 119:36-37 NKJV

TWENTY

"Point to the boys," Trent called out.

Hope stood in the back left corner of the sandy court, watching Nick as he bumped the ball from Dylan's hand and jogged into serve position. She glanced at Lexi, crouched in the back right corner ready to receive. "That point was a lucky one."

"Yeah. Call that a birthday present."

A moment later, the ball whizzed through the air to the back corner by Lexi. She passed. Hope dove for the shanked pass and bump set the ball. From her sprawled position in the sand, she saw Dylan propel himself towards the net as Lexi launched herself to hit the ball out of Dylan's reach.

"Point to the girls," Trent called out before jogging after the ball.

"Nice kill." Hope grasped the hand Lexi offered and hauled herself back to her feet. "For a moment, I thought he'd have had that one over you."

Lexi stepped closer, holding a hand against her mouth as she whispered. "I may watch YouTube beach volleyball clips to keep him on his toes."

Hope chuckled and swapped positions with Lexi, just as Dylan received the ball back from Trent. She side-eyed Lexi. "Reckon he'll jump float me?"

Lexi was focused on the other side of the net. "I'd be ready for one if I was in your place."

Dylan tossed the ball up, following it up to jump float serve. Hope sunk to her knees to dig the ball, managing to keep it up, while the wind played with the ball mid-air. Lexi set it and called for a cut shot. Hope caught Nick's approach in her periphery as she tried to cut shot the ball across the net, but her height worked against her. She landed hard in the sand as Nick spiked the ball back at her.

"Point to the boys," Trent called out.

"And that's the game." Nick strutted towards Dylan.

Hope narrowed her eyes as the boys performed an elaborate high five. "Yeah well, I'm hardly your match, Nick."

"A win's a win, Meyer."

Hope pushed herself up and dusted herself off as Lexi came alongside her. "We couldn't exactly beat the boy on his birthday now, could we?"

"Shall we go another three games?" Nick chested up to the net, passing the ball hand to hand. Lexi mirrored him. "Just. Say. When."

"Okay kids." Dylan took the ball off Nick, stooped under the net, and draped his arm over Lexi's shoulders. "It's my birthday, and I'm hungry. Let's go to dinner."

Fifteen minutes later, Hope drew in a long breath of the woodfire pizza's cooking around her. The clear calm evening held a slight chill but the temperature under the alfresco patio heaters was perfect. She smiled, listening to the conversation around her, and reflecting on the fun afternoon they'd had.

Dylan leaned forward in the chair and crossed his arms over the table. "So, Hope, how are things with you and Josh these days?"

Surprised by the question, Hope shrugged and glanced at Lexi. Hadn't she told Dylan? "Um. We broke up?"

The mood dropped, and Hope attempted a smile. "I'm ok. Think it's for the best. I mean, he never seemed to want to come to church with me."

Dylan offered a sympathetic smile back at her. "Then you'd be ok if he joins us for dinner?"

Hope choked, then cleared her throat and raised a hand to her hair. She must look a mess after volleyball.

Lexi laid her hand upon her arm. "Hope, you look fine."

"A bit rumpled, but nothing wrong with that when seeing your ex again." Nick chuckled, stretching across the table for the jug of water. Hope shot a glare at him just as a figure emerging from the pizzeria behind them caught her eye.

"Josh." Dylan stood and held his hand out. "Thanks for coming!"

"Hey, guys," Josh smiled at them all. His gaze lingered a moment on Hope before returning to Dylan. "Happy birthday, big fella." He clasped Dylan's outstretched hand.

Josh lowered himself into the seat next to Hope. His eyes seemed to shine as he looked at her. "You look a little different from the last time I saw you."

Hope smoothed out her hair, feigning a coolness she was far from feeling. "Thank you. This look is called, 'an afternoon at the beach playing volleyball.'"

Soft chuckles filled the air as she gazed back at Josh. His eyes suggested there was so much he wasn't saying. She wished they were alone. So much still needed to be said.

"It's just missing the 'we won' accessory." Nick said, breaking into her daydreaming thoughts while the others laughed.

With a droll look at Nick, Hope gave a sarcastic laugh before ordering the biggest pizza on the menu. Conversation flowed around the table just like old times, and she had to remind herself that she wasn't with Josh anymore.

"So, Josh, when are we gonna see you at church?" Lexi dropped a crust onto her plate and dusted her hands off. Hope coughed and reached for her drink, while Josh ate his last bit of pizza. Hope replaced her drink and averted her eyes. She'd asked Josh to come with her to church many times—in private. Asking in a group setting felt like an ambush.

Josh dusted off his hands. "I guess I don't see the need to go. I'm a good person. Why should I go to church when I see no difference between me and the people who go to church?"

Hope felt her eyes widen as her mind played over what Josh just said. Her heart began to thump, and her chest felt tight. Lexi answered something which the others chuckled in response to, but she didn't hear it. Everything had become white noise. She had to leave.

"Excuse me a moment, guys." Hope rose and wove her way out from the alfresco dining area. As soon as she was out of sight of the diners, she stumbled onto the narrow moonlit sandy path and followed it down to the water.

The blackened water lapped and rolled before her, highlighted by the full moon above, lulling her into a trance as she stared at it. A lump formed in her throat as she thought over what Josh had said and the part she played in his thoughts.

"Hope."

Awakened by Trent's gentle call of her name, Hope sucked in a breath. She felt his hand on her shoulder, but closed her eyes and turned from it to find she'd turned into an outstretched arm. Her eyes filled and she turned again as his arms enclosed her. She gave up as he drew her to him. Clinging to Trent's shirt, Hope allowed the tears to come.

"I'm the one he's referring to, aren't I? I'm the hypocrite?"

Trent's cultured voice reverberated in his chest beneath her ear. "Yes."

"Why? Because I'm loud and like to laugh? Because I go out and have fun?" Hope's breath shuddered and her voice sputtered like a car with a blocked fuel filter as she tried to get her words out. "Is that why he doesn't want to be with me?"

Hope pushed out of Trent's embrace and moved away from him. Hugging her arms to herself she drew in a ragged breath. "I know what the Bible says about a quiet and peaceful spirit, and I'm not that."

Trent took a step towards her. "God isn't asking everyone to have a quiet and peaceful spirit. He asks us to reflect what we know about Him, both in mind and action."

A soft breeze blew around them, and Hope hugged her arms tighter to herself. With a slight shake of her head, she looked out over the water once again. "I don't know what that looks like."

"Because of the Lord's great love, we are not consumed ..." Trent's voice enveloped Hope in warmth and she looked over at him. He was looking towards the now star-filled night sky, his expression almost longing. "... for His compassions never fail. They are new every morning."

Trent looked back at her, and Hope turned to him as she searched his face. There was something different. The hairs on the back of her neck slowly stood to attention and her arms dotted in goosebumps, but not from the cool of the night. She wasn't scared, but rather drawn by something almost mysterious she'd never glimpsed in him before.

"Tomorrow is a new day," Trent continued "Start again."

He took another step before her and held out a hand. Hope's eyes dropped to his gesture. The contours of his hand emphasized by the light of the moon, held her gaze.

"Start again." Hope murmured, her mind going at the speed of light trying to figure out what was happening.

"Tomorrow, if you like, I can take you to see Dave."

Hope nodded, then placed her hand in his before looking back at him. His warm hand closed over hers, and a peace swelled within her.

"For now, let's head back to the party before they start wondering where we are."

TWENTY-ONE

The next morning, Hope pulled up outside Dave's place next to Trent's ute and gave him a wave.

Hope gathered up her bag and stepped out of her car, thankful Trent had organized this meeting with Dave. By the time she got home for tea, some of her questions should have answers.

"How are you this morning?" Trent came alongside her as she closed the car door.

"I'm good. Keen to talk to Dave. I didn't sleep well last night. My brain kept going over what if other people feel about me the way Josh feels about me, but haven't said?"

Trent knocked on the front door. "Jump that hurdle when you get to it."

Dave's office looked different in the early hours of the day. Sunlight streamed in the open window behind the pew Dylan and Nick sat in for their leadership meetings, filling the room with the delicate scents of the potted daphnes and eucalyptus gums from their garden. Books lay open on the coffee table, and what looked to be leftover breakfast dishes and a novelty youth minister coffee cup cluttered Dave's desk.

"Come on in guys, have a seat. Excuse the mess. Early start."

Trent sat in his usual seat. Unable to resist the sunshine, Hope took a seat on the pew and looked at Dave expectedly.

Dave finished off his cuppa, rounded his desk, took a seat on the pew with Hope. "Ok, Hope. Talk to me. What's going on?"

"A number of things, but the main thing weighing on me is that I don't really know what I'm doing. Everyone seems to have a plan for life. I don't, and my ex-boyfriend thinks I'm a hypocrite."

Dave's eyebrows jumped. "Strong words. Did he say that?"

"It was implied."

"Ok. So, one problem at a time. You don't know what you're doing in what aspect? With God or in life or both?"

Hope hummed in thought. She hated sounding clueless, but she wasn't here for a chat. She wanted direction. "Both."

Dave nodded, picked up a pen and a notepad from among the books on the coffee table, and wrote something. Hope tilted her head to try and make out what he was writing. She looked over at Trent, who gave a smile of encouragement, and she turned back to Dave just as he looked back at her.

"What I propose is for you to get yourself right with God first. Then everything else will fall into place. So let's start there."

Hope took the piece of paper and read the notes he'd scrawled. Two Bible verses: Psalms 37.4 and Matt 6.33, and a website: www.discoveryourshape.org/. She looked back at him. "What is Shape?"

"Nice one, Dave."

Hope whipped her head around to look at Trent. "You know about this shape thing?"

Trent gestured back to Dave, and Hope turned back to her youth minister. There was a distinct vibe of excitement in the room, and Hope bopped on her seat. "Ok, fill me in. What is this? Where can I get it?"

"SHAPE isn't something you *get*. SHAPE is something you *are*. This website will take you to a course that's specifically designed to help each searching individual to discover themselves, then show where they can use their unique gifts and abilities in ministry."

"Huh." Hope sat back in the pew and absentmindedly studied Dave's bookcase. If this course would reveal her gifts, as Dave said, and provide direction for her, did that mean he didn't already know her gifts? Or at least suspect them? In that case, why did he ask her to be a youth leader? "Then what part do I play with the youth here? Why did you ask me to be a part of the team?"

"I think you have a tremendous gift for ministry. In exactly what area, I'm not sure yet. You could fit in a number of areas. As long as I've known you, you're always inviting people to come to church, to youth, or to activities we've planned. On top of that, you keep a lookout for visitors and make it your intention to help them feel comfortable."

"This makes you a huge target for the enemy," Dave rose and went to his bookcase. "Because you live your faith so loudly, your witness needs to be clear, or you'll send mixed messages. Was this where the hypocrite conversation came from?"

"Yes." Things were already sounding clearer, and a hazy plan was forming in her mind. She'd never considered things from that angle before.

"Now, I know you have your preferred reading genre, but try this for a change." Dave sat down beside her again and held out a book.

"*The 16 Personality Types*." Hope looked up with a frown, and Dave chuckled.

He took the piece of paper off her and scribbled something else. "If you don't want to read the book, at least do the assessment." He handed the paper back to her. He'd written the address of a website: www.16personalities.com.

Hope grinned. A breeze blew in the window behind her, and she took in a long breath of the crisp scents it brought. There was a feeling swelling inside her, and it felt a little like her name.

Hope.

TWENTY-TWO

"Hope, how was your weekend?" Claudia's voice echoed off the storeroom walls, and Hope smiled a hello to her work colleague.

"Not too bad. Yours?"

Claudia yawned and stretched her arms above her head. "Partied way too much. I tried to get out of this shift, but no one would cover me."

Hope chuckled while continuing her search through the racks of clothes for a layby a customer was waiting to pick up. "You know you're your own worst enemy, right?"

When Claudia didn't respond, Hope looked up and found her checking her phone. "Are you out here looking for something?"

Claudia shook her head. "Just checking messages. Hey, while I'm thinking about it, you free Thursday night?"

"Ah, here it is!" Hope held a garment up and lay it over her arm, then turned to Claudia with a bored expression. "Of course I'm free. The life of a single is tremendous fun."

Claudia giggled as she placed an invitation on one of the boxes. "Well, I'm having a birthday party. My best mate, Catherine, has booked a party bus and just told me." Claudia flipped her hand. "It was going to be a surprise, but she remembered I hate surprises, so she had to tell me."

Hope grinned. Claudia was very vocal about her dislike of surprises. Hope picked up the invitation and looked it over. A party bus. She had never been on one before. She hummed. "Well, Thursday nights are a good night to go out …"

"It's going to be a lot of fun. Catherine told me she's been on a few. Loads of dancing and stuff. It's all paid for, by the way."

Hope drew in a breath and sighed, quietening the faint stirring in her mind to decline the invitation. "Ok, I'll come along. Sounds like fun."

Claudia beamed. "Yay! Ok, I better get back out there. Oh … I'm off the rest of the week, so I'll see you Thursday night."

Claudia hurried from the room as Hope tucked the invitation into her back pocket. At the very least, she could say it would be an experience.

Pleased that the day was passing fast, Hope checked over the list of tasks Rob had left behind. All the things Liam requested had been ticked off, sorted, and packed away, while Rob's sat unattended. Hope's eyes hovered over Rob's list. Her eyes settled on the mundane sorting deliveries and checking off invoice jobs, when her conversation with Lexi about doing things differently came back to mind. She looked at the clock. Twenty minutes until end of shift. This would take longer than twenty minutes. With a sigh, she grabbed the list off the bench and strode out the back.

By two o'clock, Hope had finished her morning shift and wandered from the Plaza, taking in the beautiful afternoon that had settled over The Valley. She much preferred being rostered on for mornings than afternoons. Then there wasn't as much rushing around between finishing work and leadership meeting, so she could take her time and relax a bit. The sidewalks were littered with budding flowers and the air had that sweet smell about it from blossoming trees. Another sign spring was just about upon them. Her favorite season.

A car horn honked nearby, startling her from her daydreams. She looked around just as Scott's car pulled up next to her, and the passenger side window rolled down.

"Did you just do some overtime?"

Hope grinned as she hunkered down to speak through the passenger side window of Scott's car. "I did. Rob better notice."

"I doubt it. You free tonight?"

Hope's stomach fluttered, though she kept her smile in place. "Nope. Youth group meeting on Mondays. Why?"

Scott made a face of disappointment. "Need an extra on our pool table tonight. I was hoping you'd be free."

"Shooting pool isn't my kind of game. I'm more of a ball sports, running, jumping kinda gal."

"Noted." Scott chuckled before he looked over his shoulder then pulled back out into the traffic with a quick wave. Hope watched him drive off before shaking the smile off her face and crossed the road to her car. Did he just ask her out?

With a giggle to herself, Hope slipped into her car.

Hope arrived home to find everyone was out. Perfect. What Dave had asked her to do yesterday had been sitting in her mind, and she was eager to get into it. Her stomach quivered with excitement at the idea of this SHAPE program. She had never known what she wanted to do, but this program would give her at least an idea and point her in the general direction of where her strengths and skills would be useful.

After turning the coffee machine on, Hope pulled out her laptop, opened the SHAPE website, and started reading.

Two hours and three cappuccinos later, after signing up for the SHAPE program and joining their Facebook group, Hope sat back in her chair and linked her hands behind her head. That was intense. After answering a lot of in-depth questions, reading her results raised a cloud of uncertainty. The report said her gifts were giving and service, she had a passion for outreach, her strongest skills were something called interviewing and welcoming, and her personal style was unstructured—which she had to agree with.

Thankful the results had also been sent to Dave, Hope gathered up her mug and took it to the sink. She needed a run before even thinking about checking out the other resources Dave had suggested. There was enough to digest in what she'd just read. There was no need to add more.

Not yet.

Tonight, she would catch up with Dave after leadership and unravel the tangled ball of wool in her mind.

TWENTY-THREE

The evening was calm and mild for late winter as Hope made her way to Dave's. Her mind was still a flurry of thoughts and possibilities she hadn't considered before, giving her both a thrill of excitement and an uncharacteristic sense of anxiety.

Nick looked to have just arrived as Hope pulled up next to him. She stepped out of her car, then turned to greet him.

Nick beat her to it.

"Where did you and Trent take off to on Saturday night?"

Hope looked at Nick over the roof of her car as she shouldered her bag. She knew someone would bring up Saturday.

"It certainly was the elephant in the room no one wanted to address when you came back." Nick locked up his Clubsport and met her gaze.

Hope ran a hand over her hair, shrugging as she stepped alongside him. "Oh, just a little place called rock bottom."

Nick chuckled

She looked over at him. "What?"

"That's a bit dramatic, don't you think?" Nick stopped at the base of the steps leading up to Dave's porch and turned to her.

Hope paused and looked at him. "You think I'm dramatic?"

"At times, yes."

Hope blew out a humorless laugh. "Right. Ok. And you base this opinion on what?"

"One word. Dylan."

With a sniff, Hope looked down the driveway. The others would be arriving for the meeting soon. "Nick, I've already heard your theory. It's ancient history."

"Perhaps. But it has opened the door to … let's say, deeper theories."

Hope reshouldered her bag and looked at Nick with narrowed eyes. "Such as?"

"You really want me to unpack what I've gleaned about the dark recesses of Hope Meyer's mind?"

Hope crossed her arms. This will be good. "Sure. Do we need an interview room for this?"

Nick widened his stance as he pocketed his hands. "No. I started to notice a difference in you when we found out about Dylan's feelings for Lexi. The next part of my theory is based on my observations of the types of movies I know you like to watch, and books you like to read."

An uncomfortable feeling began to curl in Hope's gut. "Ok …"

"You lean towards romantic themes with strong male leads, so what Dylan did for Lexi fed into this. Some part of you wants that for yourself."

Hope stared back at Nick. Her mind turned over like a can of worms. Was she influenced by what she watched and read? Did that impact and influence the way she looked at things?

The sound of Dylan's Harley broke into her awareness and she blinked. Nick gave a light jab to her upper arm. "Don't stress about it, Meyer. Just something to keep in mind."

The roar of Dylan's Harley made a reply impossible, and Hope drew in a deep breath in of the salty night air as Dylan killed the engine, plunging them back into the silence of the evening. She waved.

Dylan took his helmet off. "Hey, guys."

"Hope, you are nailing the early discipline." Lexi called, and Hope felt a smile light her features. At least one thing about her seemed authentic.

Trent's ute appeared at the top of the driveway. As Dylan and Lexi joined Nick and herself on the porch, the door opened behind them.

"Hey, guys. Are you coming inside or are we meeting outside tonight?"

Hope greeted Dave with a smile over her shoulder, then turned back to wave at Trent. The others filed into Dave and Linda's home. Hope turned to follow.

"Hope," Trent called. "Hang on just a moment."

Hope stopped and waited as Trent close the distance between them. "You're usually inside by the time I rock up."

Trent chuckled. "You're usually late."

Hope held her hand up and Trent clasped it in a good natured high-five. "What's up?"

His expression turned from fun-loving to solemn. He remained a couple steps below her, so they were eye to eye. "The party on Thursday. Listen to your instincts on that. Don't go."

The evening breeze stirred around her as she looked back at him. Though the breeze was warm, the fine hairs on the back of her neck bristled. Did she tell him about the party bus? She narrowed her eyes at Trent. "I only just got invited. How did you know?"

He took a step up towards her. "Remember—if you intentionally put yourself on the enemy's ground, you forfeit the protection God provides."

"Are you two joining the group?" Linda's kind voice floated out from the open door behind her. A subtle change fell over Trent's expression as he smiled, then looked back at her and gestured for her to turn. Hope blinked, turned, and smiled at Linda despite the unrest she felt, then made her way toward the library. Trent was behind her, but she couldn't find her usual small talk. He had thrown her, and her intuition was screaming inside her head that something was different about him.

Trent stepped past her to open the library door, and Hope couldn't help a sideways glance as she passed him. Whatever she'd glimpsed before was gone, yet remained seared into her mind. Hope rubbed the goosebumps off her arms as she entered the library.

Dave was smiling broadly at Dylan. "What a great opportunity to use your gifts, Dylan." Dave gave a clap of his hands and relaxed back in his office chair.

"What opportunity are we talking about?" Hope asked, desperate to get her mind off its crazed trajectory.

Lexi turned to her. "You know that meeting I told you Dylan was having at the club?" she asked with a beaming smile.

Hope gasped and looked over at Dylan. "You got the job?"

Dylan grinned, clasping his hands over his thighs. "Yeah."

"That is so good. What are the details?"

"Office hours. Weekends free. Some training involved, but nothing too hard. Definitely didn't expect my life to head in this direction, but I'm really looking forward to the challenge."

While thrilled for Lexi, Hope was aware of the twinge inside her mind. Dylan knew what he was doing and was headed in that direction. That meant everyone in the room except her knew what God wanted them to do in life.

Dear God, please let this SHAPE program be pointing me in the right direction. Please.

"Ok all, let's get back to the meeting." Dave chuckled while reshuffling papers over his desk. "First up. Trent, Lexi. Where are we at with the outreach excursion?"

"It's all teed up for Friday week." Trent relaxed in his seat. "Lexi and I have spoken about consent forms and have drafted one up—"

"Oh, shoot. Sorry, Trent. I was supposed to email that to Dave." Lexi looked at Dave before making a note on her paper. "I'll email that through tonight when I get home."

Dave nodded. "Fantastic. We'll announce it to the youth on Friday night, and they'll have a week to decide if they wanted to be a part of it and get the consent forms back to us.

The rest of the meeting went by in a blur. Worries about the planned outreach and what the SHAPE results meant continued to circle her mind. The clock on Dave's wall looked to be moving at glacial pace. Hope doodled on her notepad to give the illusion she was paying attention and taking notes, yet all she seemed to have written down was Beatitudes. She'd have to play catch-up with the crew before Friday night.

At last, Dave brought the meeting to a close. Hope hung back while everyone filed out, eager to talk to Dave. The sounds of her friends' vehicles leaving echoed in the quiet of the night.

"I got your SHAPE results this afternoon," Dave said before she could say anything. "I've looked them over. What were your thoughts?"

"Honestly? I was confused and surprised." Hope lifted a shoulder.

"I wasn't. But I can say I'm clearer about what direction you may enjoy going in."

A black cloud seemed to blow away in Hope's mind. Keen for some direction in life, she took a seat on the edge of the couch. "Really? That's great. What do you think?"

"Let's say, I think you'll get more out of the homeless shelter visit than you expect."

A lopsided grin curled on Hope's mouth as she considered what Dave might not be saying. He had a way of wanting them to figure things out for themselves, and she had the distinct feeling he was taking this approach with her now.

But what was it?

TWENTY-FOUR

ope looked up and down the street again.

Claudia said the party bus would pick her up at the Valley Train Station at seven-thirty. The bus was now eleven minutes late. Why was she going when she really didn't want to? She should have declined. Gone with her gut.

Listened to Trent.

Just then, a hot pink double-decker bus appeared around the corner, covered in graffiti detail and lit up like a Christmas tree. The bus slowed down to pick her up, and Claudia appeared at the door. "Hey! Sorry we're late. Come and join the party."

After greeting the driver, Hope looked around the club on wheels. To her left was a spiral staircase to the top level, and the lower deck looked just like a bus except for the party lighting. Following Claudia up the spiral staircase, Hope stepped onto the second level and couldn't believe what she was seeing. The seats were against the windows, and the rest of the space was empty except for two central poles and a small bar at the back.

"This is nuts!" Hope grabbed a pole to steady herself as the bus lurched into gear and the music started pumping.

Claudia flashed Hope a brilliant smile. "Come and sit. I want to introduce you to some people."

"Ok, Hope," Claudia said, "This is Lisa, Catherine, and Rowan."

Hope smiled at each of them in greeting, although straight away she noticed the lack of interest Rowan was showing to the seductive strokes of Catherine's fingernails along his arm.

The bus came to a stop after a while. Hope looked out the window to see where they were, and cringed.

Claudia laughed and dragged her to her feet just as a pair of large hands clamped over her shoulders. She cast a look behind her.

"C'mon." Rowan stooped to speak against her ear, his deep voice a husky drawl. "It might be better than it looks." Doubtful—there wasn't even a name for the club out the front.

Hope snickered. As she descended the stairs, Rowan's fingers gave her shoulders a rub.

They entered the club, and Hope realized this was going to be a slow night. The club was fairly empty, the DJ hadn't set up yet, and the lights weren't even turned down. How long were they going to spend at this place?

With no inspiration to dance, Hope perched herself at the bar and ordered a can of coke, watching the rest of the party mingle and dance.

Claudia appeared beside her. "You having fun?"

Hope flashed a grin. "Always. You?"

Claudia shook her head. "Not really. I want to go to the next place, so I'm rallying the troops. Finish ya drink." She picked up her drink and moved away to speak to each of her party guests, then signaled toward the door for everyone to head back to the bus.

The second club was one Hope had been to before, and her mood lifted the moment she stepped through the doors. The DJ had the dance floor full, and the colored strobe light effects gave the impression everyone was moving in slow motion. People lined the bar four deep with animated faces, standing close together to speak over the music, while the DJ looked cool and calm playing up to the throngs before him.

Hope needed no encouragement to hit the dance floor here. No sooner had she stepped onto the hardwood floor than one of her favorite dance songs started thumping through the bass and reverberating up her spine. Lost in the music, Hope closed her eyes and let the music move her while she sang along to "From Paris to Berlin." When she opened her eyes, she smiled at Claudia and Lisa who had joined her. A body pushed in on her right, and Hope turned to see Rowan moving in on their dance space.

Confidence oozed from him as he moved in closer. The girls forgotten, Hope turned herself to him. His eyes gleamed and Hope held his gaze as the hypnotic rhythm enveloped them. She knew they were moving in sync—she could feel it—so wasn't surprised when Rowan's hands found their way around the curve of her back and drew her into him. Hope slid her arms around his neck, relishing the unspoken conversation their bodies were having. When Rowan dipped his head and ran his mouth along her jaw, a heat rocketed through Hope and she moved into his advance, anticipating the moment his lips would find hers.

"Hope!" A hand tapped on her shoulder.

Spell broken, Rowan pulled back. Hope turned to look at Claudia, swallowing her irritation at being interrupted. Her hands slipped from around Rowan's neck and he loosed his hands from her waist.

"What's up?" Hope shouted over the music, keeping the annoyance she felt out of her voice. Claudia indicated to follow, then turned and disappeared with Lisa into the crowds of people towards the ladies' rest rooms.

The bathroom floors were sticky, the air was dank, and florescent lights flickered over the basins. Hope let the door swing shut behind her. Claudia and Lisa exchanged a look before looking at her. Hope lifted her shoulders, annoyance still bubbling in her blood. "Everything ok?"

Lisa cringed and Claudia rubbed her arms as if she was cold. "Rowan has a girlfriend."

The quiet in the room lengthened and Hope pressed her mouth into a thin line. Equal parts irritated and sad, she looked between the two girls. "What?"

Claudia continued. "He's with Catherine."

Hope blinked. "I had no idea."

Claudia touched her arm. "I told her that. Maybe keep a distance from him for the rest of the night?"

"Easy done." Hope spat out a laugh then turned to leave the toilets.

The rest of the night was lackluster. While the party continued, Hope just wanted to go home. She shouldn't have come. She should have listened to her intuition—like Trent said. When Claudia signaled everyone back to the bus, Hope was first on board.

Hope sat downstairs with the tired partygoers. Rowan headed upstairs, gesturing for her to follow him. She shook her head as she turned away. She'd managed to avoid him in the last two clubs, so now she just had to get through the ride home, and she could put the night behind her.

"Hey, you. I thought you'd taken a taxi home," Claudia shouted, leaning over the seat in front of Hope.

Hope's mouth tipped on one side. "Nar, just keeping my distance."

Claudia rolled her eyes. "Come upstairs. It's boring down here."

Hope flicked her hand to dismiss the invitation, but Claudia grabbed her arm and tugged her out of the seat. "It's my birthday, and I want to party until the last!"

Upstairs, the bus was in full party mode. Lights flashed and everyone was dancing with drinks in hand. Hope stood beside the top of the spiral stairs and leaned against the handrail, gripping it against the rock of the traveling bus.

"I'll get you a drink." Claudia wove her way back through the packed top floor of the bus, while Hope watched some drunk girls attempt seductive pole dancing moves on the bus's center poles.

Why had she agreed to come along to this night in the first place?

"I thought you'd gone." Rowans gravelly voice was too close. Hope started then shrank back. She smiled back at him, but her mind held a steady bass beat. Jerk, jerk, jerk, jerk.

"Had a fun night?" Rowan leaned into her, so close she could feel his stubbled jaw move against her cheek as he spoke over the music. She lifted her shoulder in a half-shrug, careful to keep her expression neutral.

The bus lurched. Rowan grabbed the rail behind Hope with one hand to steady himself, then used his position as excuse to lean closer to her. Hope leaned backwards as his other hand found the railing on her other side. He said something through a lopsided grin as his weight over her increased and the small of her back found the curve of the rail behind her as she turned her face away from him.

The bus rounded a corner, forcing more of Rowan's weight onto her and curving her further over the rail. With a yelp, Hope let her grip of the rail go and grabbed onto Rowan's shirt. His arm came around her waist and he pulled her up as the bus began to slow.

The music turned down and a voice came over the sound system. "The Valley Train Station."

As Hope disengaged herself from Rowan and headed back down the stairs, she caught Claudia watching her. The girl's expression said it all.

What on earth was that?

TWENTY- FIVE

*H*ope raked a hand through her hair. No, last night was not a nightmare. It had actually happened. The look on Claudia's face was imprinted on her brain and had featured in every dream she'd had during her fitful sleep.

With a long, heavy sigh, Hope pushed herself up and shuffled to her wardrobe. Work started in just under an hour, and her reasons for leaving were mounting.

With no appetite, she passed on breakfast and drove straight to work. She was starting to enjoy the discipline of being early or on time. Plus, this way, she could catch Claudia and get the whole thing sorted out before work started.

The car park held a sprinkle of early shopper cars, but none of them were Claudia's, so Hope parked and waited. She looked at her phone: ten minutes until she had to clock on. She drummed her fingers on the steering wheel, trying to think about what to say. Claudia's car pulled up a few parks down from her, and Hope pushed open her car door and was crossing the parking lot before Claudia had climbed out of her car.

"Hi, Claudia."

Claudia looked up, her eyes widened before shuttering and her head dropped. Her silence was a worry, but Hope rounded her friend's car and came alongside her just as Claudia turned towards the plaza.

"Claudia, I need to talk to you." Hope matched her pace to Claudia's as Claudia seemed to be hurrying.

Claudia sighed.

"What? You're not talking to me? Why? Did I kill someone last night? C'mon."

"You might not have killed anyone last night, but you did kill something." Claudia adjusted the bag hanging off her shoulder and pushed through the Bridgeshore Plaza doors.

Hope laid a hand on her arm. "Whoa. What did I kill?"

Claudia stopped and finally looked at her. "A relationship. Rowan broke up with Catherine."

Hope's stomach churned. Was Claudia trying to lay blame for this at her feet? "And that's because of me how?"

Claudia coughed a laugh. "Oh, you're next level. You know that?"

Claudia hurried off toward the staff room. Hope looked after her a moment before following, choosing not to say anything more until they got to their lockers. This was absurd.

Murmuring voices and the shutting of lockers greeted Hope and Claudia as they entered the staff room. Colleagues were finishing morning coffees and breakfast bars, and carried on as though no one had entered the room. Hope pulled up next to Claudia's locker and felt her jaw lock as she eyed her workmate. "Ok, spill. What is going on?"

Claudia shoved her bag into her locker and huffed as she slammed the door. "You're seriously going to pretend you had nothing to do with it?"

Hope gapped at Claudia. "Oh, I know I didn't. From what I saw of those two, that fire was long gone out."

"And you thought, because you're single now, you'd just move on in and put the last nail in the coffin?" A subtle snarl ghosted over Claudia's expression.

Hope smarted. "Absolutely not! I'm saying I tried to avoid him after you told me he was with Catherine. What you saw was him leaning me over the bus handrail so far that when the bus turned a corner, I thought I was going to fall backward. I grabbed onto him, and that was when he grabbed me. Until that moment I wasn't touching him or even talking to him."

Claudia rolled her eyes and turned away with a sardonic laugh. "Oh, please."

"Why don't you believe me?" Hope pleaded as Claudia disappeared down the hall then turned towards the floor.

Hope shifted her weight and took a few moments before heading out onto the floor herself. Rowan had been all over her. What on earth did Claudia think she had done wrong?

It was going to be a long shift.

* * * *

When Hope entered the hall for youth night, the boys were setting out trestle tables and Dave was carrying boxes from out behind the stage.

As anticipated, the afternoon had dragged on. Claudia avoided her at every opportunity, giving them no time to talk, and the customers seemed to be extra taxing. With a heavy sigh, Hope put a smile on her face and made her way over to Dave to ask how she could help with setting up.

Hearing the door open, Hope looked up to see Trent enter the room, and his warning to not go on the party bus came back to mind. She groaned inwardly. How she wished she'd taken that advice …or better, gone with her gut and declined the invitation in the first place.

"Evening, Hope. How has your week been?" Dave called over his shoulder as she approached.

Hope shrugged. "Better than some. Can I give you a hand?"

Dave chuckled and nodded in a knowing way. "I know that feeling well. You're being challenged to see life differently, and it can rattle you."

"That's for sure—"

Behind them, the hall doors burst open with the first of the teens charging in. Hope forgot what she was going to say as she looked over at their animated faces.

"Hope, Hope, Hope! Hey!"

Curious to know what the teens wanted to talk to her about, Hope forgot about her terrible day and focused on their radiant expressions. Their energy emitted from them as they approached, their voices blending together as they all tried to talk at once, telling her about their week, things they'd done, movies they'd watched, places they'd been, when Lexi and Trent appeared behind them.

With a quick glance at Trent, Hope held her hands up and chuckled. "One at a time. I can't hear you."

"Maybe save it until café, everyone" Trent said from behind the youth crowding her. "Let's get this night started." Trent gave a clap of his hands, then gestured over his shoulder towards where the icebreaker was about to start.

The girls turned to head back to the group when Melanie looked over her shoulder. "Hope, before we go home tonight, you gotta show us that dance move you were doing with that guy last night!"

Hope felt her mouth drop open as Jade turned and walked backwards, her eyes held a mischievous glint. "Oh, yeah. Yeahhh. That looked hot as."

Melanie nudged Jade with her shoulder, and Jade turned back to the group, her laugh floating over her shoulder and she shared smiles with the other girls. Hope felt her face boom with color as the girls walked away.

Mouth dry, Hope licked her lips and swallowed hard, a million thoughts fighting it out in her mind. She became aware of Lexi and Trent's eyes upon her. The look on their faces mirrored her own feeling: she had smashed her witness.

TWENTY-SIX

Hope yawned into her palm. Normally she loved being trackside on Sunday afternoon, watching her little brother train. They had always been close, and she was his biggest supporter. But today she didn't want to go.

Weighed down by her thoughts, she sighed and yawned again. The dance with Rowan kept playing over in her mind, and now she felt ill knowing at least two nineteen-year-olds she knew through church had been watching her. She could barely look anyone in the eye the rest of youth on Friday night and she'd even skipped church. She could only imagine how that dance would have looked. Now she didn't know how to be at church in front of those girls, with them having that image of her in their minds.

Hope stood, desperate for reprieve from the downward spiral she knew she was on.

"Ok, I need a drink," she muttered as she scanned the food and beverage trailers scattered around the dirt track. There was

the potato van, and right next door was a coffee van. "Jacket potatoes. Yes, come at me."

As Hope made her way over to the food area, her thoughts
about food were quickly overshadowed by thoughts about
Claudia. She was so angry at Hope over the party bus night, and
the other girls seemed distant as well.

The smell of buttery baked potatoes quickly stomped out the
gloomy thoughts. Hope licked her lips as she ordered a super-
sized jacket potato with the lot, a pink iced doughnut, and an
extra tall cappuccino.

Once seated cross-legged on the lawn, Hope began to indulge
in her lunch while she watched the dirt bikes jump and perform
stunts as they went round the track.

"Hope?"

Hope whipped her head towards the male voice. The only
person close to her was a helmeted rider who was taking off his
gloves and looking in her direction. She smiled, dusting off her
hands. Obviously, he knew her.

"Hey," she called back, with a wave of her hand. A low
chuckle emanated from behind the helmet as the rider pocketed
his gloves then loosened the helmet strap under his chin.

"You have no idea who I am, do you?"

"Nope, but that doesn't change my manners." Hope lifted a
shoulder and grinned as she popped another chip in her mouth.

The rider pulled his helmet off and tucked it under his arm.
"Surprised to see me here?"

Hope coughed, almost choking on the chip. "Liam! I didn't
know you rode."

His riding attire emphasized his broad shoulders and narrow
waist, the boots made him look even taller, and his dark blue eyes
shone with a hunger of competitiveness she often saw in the rid-
ers' when they came off the tracks.

"I've been racing for years." Liam said. "But only re-joined
this club recently. Why are you here?"

Hope gestured to the track. "See the skinny little guy in blue and black. Red dirt bike?"

Liam looked over at the track and hummed.

"That's Ryan, my little brother."

"He's a good racer." Liam turned back to look at her, his smile one she'd never glimpsed at work. "Very impressed with his style."

Hope smiled up at Liam. For some reason, knowing he thought Ryan was a good rider made her happy. Ryan needed a strong male figure to lavish praise upon him, since Dad was always busy. "You should tell him that."

Liam ran a hand over his head. "I will. I better head back. I just needed to grab a bite to eat and thought I'd come over and say g'day when I saw you sitting over here."

"No worries. See you at work." Hope lifted a hand to wave him off when she saw a question cross his features. He moved his helmet into his other hand and unhooked his sunglasses from his racing jersey. "I didn't see you at Jenny's party last night. Did your church have something on?"

Hope couldn't help the frown that crinkled her brow. She'd never heard of a party at Jenny's. "No, sorry. I was just hanging out at home. What party?"

It was unmissable. The look of dropping someone in it was written all over his face. Liam made a dismissive face and put on his sunglasses. "Oh, right. Not sure what happened there, I thought everyone was invited, but it was kind of last minute. Sorry to leave you on that note, Hope, but I better head back."

Liam lifted a hand and turned back to the food vans. Hope watched him go, an uncomfortable sensation settling in her stomach. Why would the girls leave her out? Did they leave her out deliberately, or was it an oversight? She'd ask Claudia on her next shift, but felt deep within this had something to do with the party bus.

A roar of dirt bikes filled the air, drawing Hope from her inward thoughts and back to the racetrack. She checked her phone for the time and tried to focus on the practice race. Only an hour to go, then they could leave.

A beep sounded from her bag. Hope drew her bag over to her to fish out her phone. Dragging her eyes from the race in progress, she flicked open her phone to see she'd received a message from Nick. Hope fumbled her phone in haste several times until she grabbed the phone in a death grip and opened the message.

'Hey all, who's available for a quick catchup?'

Hope's stomach flipped. She hit reply.

'Sure, I'm free. Can be there in an hour.'

Waiting for a reply message is as bad as waiting for a coffee machine to make a drink. The roar of dirt bikes and conversations from the pits filled the late afternoon air as Hope watched her phone, waiting for Nick's reply to come through. When her phone finally beeped, she had the message open before the second beep.

'See you then'.

Hope slumped back against her elbows on the cooling lawn and placed her phone back in her bag. Finally, an opportunity to discuss what had been happening.

Hopefully it was good news, news that her friends were safe and all was being resolved.

She really needed to hear something positive at the moment.

TWENTY- SEVEN

ope arrived at Nick's place. There were no other cars there. Maybe because it was an impromptu catch up. Maybe the others were held up.

Hope knocked on the door and took in the street around her as she pulled her cardigan tighter around her. The sun was sitting low on the horizon, and the neighborhood kids were playing football in the street. The door opened behind her.

"Hey, thanks for coming." Nick stood back and held the door open. "The others couldn't make it."

Hope flashed Nick a smile as she stepped inside the cozy warmth of the loungeroom. "That's cool." She shrugged out of her cardigan and took a seat at the rustic mammoth stone bar Nick's dad had built into the room.

Nick rounded the bar, took out two glasses, and placed them on the bar mat in front of her. "Coke?"

Hope nodded as she hung her cardigan off the back of the high-back bar stool. "So tell me, what's up? Not like you to hold an impromptu gathering."

A hiss filled the air as Nick cracked a bottle of Coke open, then filled the two glasses. "We've found the offender who tried to get the wind up you and Lexi. Turns out the big fella had ahh … a wannabe stalker."

Hope frowned back at Nick, watching him take a sip of his drink. "A stalker …?"

Nick swallowed his mouthful. "I know. Who'd stalk Dylan?"

With a roll of her eyes Hope readjusted herself on the stool before taking a sip of her drink. "I thought stalkers stalked their target. Is this guy, lost?"

A whisper of a smile tickled the corners of Nick's mouth as he raised his drink to take a sip. "Not quite. He claims he didn't know where Dylan lived, so he went with what he knew in the hopes of flushing him out."

"How do you know this guy is telling the truth?"

"Simple." Nick rounded the bar and took a seat next to Hope, the ice in his drink tinkling against the glass he held. "We have a team watching the people Jack was associated with. All we need is one more piece of evidence to bag them altogether and we can throw the book at them. So when I gave the team the information you and Lexi had given me, they just checked it against the surveillance they had, and it didn't line up. We knew the guy you both saw was a stalker." Nick grinned into his drink. "Wasn't hard to catch him, either."

Hope gave a slow nod as Nick emptied his glass. Either way, reading between the lines, the guy still must be a loose cannon. She shivered.

"So no more 'visits' then?"

Nick shook his head. "No more visits, no more jumping at shadows."

"Hmm. You're so empathetic. Thanks." Hope fiddled with her half-empty glass, spinning it over the rubbery bar mat, focusing on the way the dark liquid rolled around the inside of the glass. There was a crazy person out there who knew where to find her, Claudia was acting strange towards her since the party bus, and she still had no idea what direction her life was headed in.

A light cuff to her upper arm brought her attention back to Nick.

"What's up, Meyer?"

Hope drew in a long breath and sighed. "Oh, nothing. Just heard some other stuff today that's sitting heavy in my head."

Nick looked back at her as if he was waiting for more information. Hope stopped rolling her glass around on the rubber mat.

"It's ok, Nick. I won't bore you with details. I just need to talk to Lexi. She's a bit warmer than you."

Nick placed his glass on the bar mat and rested an elbow on the counter. "Good to hear."

Hope wrinkled her nose as she glared at him.

Nick chuckled. "Easy there, tiger."

"Well, she would have at least hugged me by now."

"Ok. I'll do my best Lexi impersonation." Nick straightened on his seat and plastered a big smile on his face. "What's up, girlfriend?" he asked in a bad falsetto.

"Oh, stop." Hope slapped at him, trying to contain a chuckle. Nick sat back in his seat and laughed.

The fire crackled away, deliciously warming Hope's back as she looked back at Nick. He'd been right about a number of other things about her, so maybe he could help her with the issue with Claudia.

"Alright. You wanna know what's up? Well, I went to a party on Thursday night. Some guy hits on me and since I'm single now, I was all for it. Then I found out he had a girlfriend, so, I avoided him the rest of the night. However, as fate seems to have it—for me—we ended up in a bit of a compromising position, which my friend from work saw. Now she's gone cold on me and somehow this has filtered through work, and I didn't get invited to a party last night ..."

The front door handle rattled. Nick's mum entered, bags of groceries hanging off her forearms. "Hi Nick. Oh, hi Hope. How are you? How are your folks?"

Though flustered by the interruption, Hope hid it and waved at Nick's mum as she approached. "Hey, Mrs. Marshall. We're all good, thanks. How are you?"

Nick rose and unhooked some bags off his mum's arm, then followed her to the kitchen. Mrs. Marshall chatted about everything she'd been doing while unpacking the bags. Nick returned and gave a head nod towards the front door.

Hint received.

Hope waited for Mrs. Marshall to finish her story before she rose from her stool and dragged her cardigan with her. "Sorry, Mrs. Marshall. I've got to head off. Good to see you."

Mrs. Marshall waved from the kitchen. "You too, Hope. Sorry to have missed your visit."

Nick opened the door and gestured for Hope to head out first. "She'll be back, Mum. I'll book you in with her next time."

The sound of Mrs. Marshall's laughter faded as Nick closed the front door behind them.

Despite the cold nip in the air, it was a beautiful evening with the Milky Way twinkling right over The Valley. Hope pulled her cardigan on and hugged it tight around her while looking up at the stars. She never got tired of looking at the night sky.

"You were saying?" Nick came alongside her.

Hope felt his intense gaze and tore her eyes from the Southern Cross constellation to look back at him. "Huh? Oh. Ah, yeah. The work thing. On top of that, two girls I know from youth were at the club that night, and they saw me with the guy."

"Is that the real reason you didn't come to church yesterday?"

Hope shot Nick a guilty look then looked back at the stars. "I couldn't look those girls in the eyes, you know." She heard Nick clear his throat and braced herself for what was coming. His insights were often brutal.

"Tell me, if they hadn't seen you, would you have still come to church?"

Hope frowned and turned back to face him. Where was he going with this? "I guess so …"

A long moment passed before Nick's stern expression turned playful. He rubbed the back of his head before letting his hand fall to his side. "You really don't see it, do you?"

"See what?" Hope felt defensiveness rise within her, adrenaline simmered beneath the surface of her control, and she squared herself to Nick. He seemed to be struggling to find words—for once. Tilting her head at him, she waited, training her hardest stare upon him.

Nick linked his hands behind his head and moved a few paces away. She could hear his sigh. Whatever he wanted to say must be brutal, if he was taking this long to get the words out.

"Will you just say it?"

Nick turned. "Do you see the hypocrisy of your actions? It's probably what Josh was trying to tell you about—I read between the lines at dinner the other week—when he called the break on your relationship. I'm guessing it's the same issue with the girls at work. They see you one way at a party, then you're off to help run a youth group program at church."

Staring back at Nick, Hope blinked.

"I think part of you must understand this," Nick continued, "Because—by your own admission—you would have come to church if the youth from church hadn't seen you. Stands to reason that you're aware on some level that your behavior wasn't consistent for someone claiming to be a Christian."

Hope took a step back, unsure what to say. She felt close to tears and needed to sit. Instead, finding her car, she leaned back against it. "I was just having some fun." Her voice was just above a whisper.

Nick took a step towards her. "I know. You're one of the most fun people I know. I don't say this to upset you, but to wake you up. Life isn't a series of fictional scripts you watch or read. Life is what happened to Lexi or what's going on with Dylan's family or attending a car accident and finding the driver smeared over the road …"

Nick fell silent and Hope watched him look away. Lost for words, she took in his profile while the evening silence rang in her ears. The lock of his jaw, the bob of his Adam's apple and the slow draw in of a long breath told her he was only just in control. He was talking about something he'd seen. She felt punched in the gut and took a step towards him.

"Nick, I'm—"

"I'm ok." Nick held a hand up but didn't look at her. "Had some counseling to process it, but that's beside the point. I'm not trivializing your issue. I just hope you can see the problem staring you right in the face. There are bigger issues out there, and people need hope. How can they find hope when the people holding hope dilute it or even hide it?"

An uncomfortable feeling began to weave its way into Hope's mind as she took in Nick's strained profile. She'd had no idea—hadn't even considered—the things he must have seen since leaving the academy. She'd never even asked him how he was going. She felt ashamed.

The silence stretched between them like a wet blanket. There was only one thing she could do now. With a push off her car, Hope closed the distance between them and without a word, enclosed Nick in an embrace.

"Thank you. For everything."

TWENTY-EIGHT

Hope's slippers scuffed loudly on the floating floorboards as she made her way into the kitchen for a morning cuppa.

"Sleep well?" Ryan's voice entered her fuzzy thoughts, and she looked sluggishly across the room at him. A humorless smile lifted a corner of her mouth. "Morning, bro. I did … until I had a horrible dream. Then couldn't get back to sleep."

Hope dropped a double espresso pod into the coffee machine and set it to start before stretching over the kitchen bench with a groan. The conversation with Nick from last night still played over in her mind. She heard Ryan's chuckle and opened an eye.

"Shut up, you."

With great effort, Hope turned her attention back to the coffee machine. Once her mug was full, she took it over to the breakfast table and sat heavily. She pulled out her phone to check her job search app again.

Maybe today would be her lucky day.

*   *   *   *

Ambling into work with the knowledge her colleagues were excluding her was an odd feeling. The smiles, the greetings, the friendly chitchat while passing through departments to the staff room, what was that about? Lies or her own delusion?

Hope put her things in her locker and shut the steel door with a clang. It was an obvious slip from Liam about the party but, what if he hadn't slipped? How many other things might be going on that she wasn't told about? Was it just her work colleagues, or did it extend beyond work?

Hope rubbed her arms as she headed out of the staff room. This was an odd feeling.

Resolved this was not going to affect her, Hope squared her shoulders back and greeted everyone she passed just like any other day, as she wove her way towards the changeroom. Claudia was sorting a pile of discarded clothing.

"Hey, Claudia," Hope said in a singsong voice as she swanned into the room. She picked an item up off the floor and flopped it back onto Claudia's pile before straightening up the curtains in the changing cubicles.

"Hi." Claudia's tone was distant, and her attention remained on the pile of clothes. Hope turned and narrowed her eyes on her workmate. Claudia was either ignoring her now or was deep in thought. Well, Hope hated mincing words. She'd get straight to the point—via a little subterfuge.

"How was your weekend? How was Jenny's par-tay?"

Claudia's head jerked up. Hope met her surprised look with her most enthusiastic expression, and watched her colleague try to smile before she returned her gaze back to work. "Ah, yeah. Party was great. So sad I didn't see you there though."

"I couldn't make it," Hope lied. "Was everyone there?"

Claudia shot Hope a look that told her she was uncomfortable and her pretense was failing, as did Claudia's quick glance to the right—revealed that she was about to make up a story. Hope joined her at the folding table and picked up an item to rehang. Claudia didn't have enough imagination to whip up a believable lie on the spot, so she kept a smile on her face and continued working.

Eventually, Claudia sighed. "Ok. Who told you?"

Hope looked up and blinked. She was not expecting Claudia to cave that fast. She shook her head and feigned confusion. "Who told me what?"

"Jenny's party. Who told you?"

"Was I not supposed to know?" Hope put down the garment and glared at Claudia. They had worked together for years. Since when did the girl stab her in the back? Claudia looked to be struggling to find any words and wouldn't look at her.

Hope's mouth tightened as long seconds ticked by.

Liam entered the storeroom, his eyes on the tablet in his hands. He looked to be marking something off.

"Alright ladies, we've just had about three weeks of back orders finally arrive, and the storeroom is overflowing." He looked up. "How are we going in here?"

His gaze darted between the both of them as if he'd read the tension in the room. Hope tossed her hair and smiled. "Great. We're almost finished here, so I can help out the back if you need me?".

"Yes, please. I've got a few more things to organize, then I'll head out the back and help you with the sorting." Liam clicked the stylus back in place and turned to leave.

Once Liam was out of earshot, Hope looked back at Claudia. Claudia was eyeballing her like a hawk watching its prey.

"Liam told you, didn't he?"

Hope straightened. "Doesn't matter who told me. The real question is why wasn't I invited?"

Claudia sniffed and went back to the table of discarded clothing, moving the items around without hanging anything. Hope glared at the top of Claudia's head for a moment. Her stomach knotted.

"What's going on? Why am I being left out?"

Claudia's manic handling of clothing stilled, and she sighed before lifting her head. "You seriously don't know?"

"I wouldn't be asking if I knew."

"Ok. Well, it was my idea to throw Jenny a party and quite frankly, I didn't want you there after seeing you in action at my party."

Claudia went back to sorting clothes, but now in an unhurried manner. Whatever was bugging her was now off her chest—and laden onto Hope's. Hope rubbed her sternum. Something hurt inside.

Hope cleared her throat and looked up at the fluorescent lights lining the ceiling. "Seen me in action?"

Claudia fed a blouse onto a hanger then hung it up. "Have you forgotten Rowan so quickly? Oh, of course you have, because Liam is waiting for you out the back."

Hope's face burned. She knew what Claudia meant, but Claudia was wrong. Hope stepped up to the workbench, her hand on the shirt Claudia was about to thread onto the hanger.

"Rowan was coming onto me the whole night," Hope said in a low tone, struggling to keep her voice controlled.

"Oh please. I saw your moves with him on the dance floor, and you wonder why I've never come along to your church."

Hope stepped back from the table, feeling as though she'd been struck. "What?"

"Why would I? You're supposed to be a Christian but you dance like that with a total stranger?" Claudia finished hanging the last item then wiped down the bench. "Seems to me that the only difference between us is I don't pretend I'm better than anyone else."

Before Hope could answer, Claudia rounded the bench and left the changeroom. A million thoughts clashed in her mind in the quiet of the dressing rooms, though none more so than how closely Claudia's words echoed Josh's.

Remember what the Bible says about stumbling blocks.

Hope turned and slumped against the bench at the memory—something Lexi had said to her after she had been flirting with Shaun at the basketball game. She sniffed in self-deprecation as she pushed herself off the bench to make her way out the back. Back then she saw it as fun, but now her version of fun was being questioned—as Dave said would happen.

Hope began opening the packages, the rip of the sticky tape off the boxes echoing around the storeroom's concrete floors and walls. Lexi had tried to warn her that day and Hope had brushed her friend off. Maybe others had also warned her. Maybe Josh ending their relationship was the wake-up call she needed.

Was she a stumbling block? A bad example?

Hope leant over the pellet of goods and dropped her head into her hands.

She was a mess.

TWENTY-NINE

The Ocean View café, Lexi's workplace, was quiet. Scattered afternoon diners sat around the food court while eighties music piped over the radio. Lexi was restocking the fridges as Hope perched on a stool at the bench. She waited until Lexi turned around before saying anything.

Hope still wasn't sure how to introduce what she wanted to talk about. She just knew she needed to talk. She traced a fingernail over the woodgrain countertop, following the age lines in the timber when her gaze zeroed in on her fingernail. Perfectly shaped and polished. She held her hand up and looked at her nails.

"Thinking about your next manicure?"

A sardonic grin twisted on Hope's mouth as she lifted her eyes to Lexi. The chuckle that exited her echoed the dullness she felt inside. "No. Surprisingly."

Lexi leant over the counter and clasped her hands. "What's up?"

"Am I a bad example? You know, in a Christian way?"

Lexi laughed and shook her head. Hope could tell she was shocked by the question and blunt delivery, but there was no point in small talk and Lexi was at work, so they could be interrupted any moment.

Then a frown crinkled Lexi's brow and she held up a finger. "Oh wait … hang on. Sometimes. When you flirted with Dylan at the movie night at church earlier this year, and with Shaun at … well, anytime you see him really. Why are you asking?"

The tightness in Hope's chest returned, and she turned her eyes back to the countertop at the memories Lexi's words conjured up. She slumped on the stool. She didn't need a mirror to know her eyes were dull, and she was beginning to understand it did in fact take more muscles to frown than to smile. She rubbed her cheeks. "Well, the girls at work apparently think I am."

Lexi turned and pulled a double chocolate cheesecake out from the fridge and placed it in front of Hope. "Here. It's on the house. I thought you got along well with the girls at work. What changed?"

Hope took the spoon Lexi handed her, and took a spoonful of the velvety smooth dessert. She relished the way cheesecake melted over her tongue, the way its sweet and creamy taste filled her mouth, She closed her eyes and sighed. "Mmm, this is so good. What was I talking about again?"

"Whatever it was can't be that bad."

Hope started at the male voice and opened her eyes to see Trent settle himself on a stool next to her. She covered her mouth, feeling a cough coming as crumbs from the cheesecake base tickled the back of her throat.

Trent smiled at her a moment before turning to Lexi. "Lexi, could I please grab a chamomile tea?"

Hope swallowed her mouthful, and while still covering her mouth, used her tongue to ensure all evidence of chocolate cheesecake was gone from her teeth. "What are you doing here?"

Lexi placed a large mug in front of Trent, along with a teapot and infuser. Steam wisped from the mug as Trent placed the infuser in the pot. "I was on my way home and thought I'd swing by. I see you're eating cheesecake ..."

Hope rolled her eyes, ignoring the odd sensation stirring within her chest at his sudden appearance. "Yes, Trent. I'm comfort eating. But Lexi made me."

Lexi mock-gasped before turning away to continue restocking the fridges, although she didn't manage to hide her grin.

"Ask Hope why I gave her the cheesecake."

Hope opened her mouth to defend herself when Trent held up a hand. "I know it's Lexi's desire to help, and it's against your nature to say no."

Hope pointed her spoon at Trent. "Only to cheesecake."

Another chuckle came from the general direction of the fridge, and Hope glared at the back of Lexi's head.

"Hope." Trent's voice interrupted Hope's planned retort. "Tell me, what's got you digging into that cheesecake like it's the last plate of cheesecake that will ever be?"

The counter bell chimed, and Lexi disappeared to serve the customer. Hope knew Trent was looking at her, his gaze always held a warmth that she felt. She looked back at him. "The girls at work have issues with me and don't want me around anymore."

"Why do you think that is?"

"You remember what those girls said at youth group last week, about me dancing with some guy?"

Trent gave a slow nod of his head and Hope dropped her gaze. She still couldn't believe how bad that night had turned. "Well, that happened at the party you somehow knew I was going to, and the guy had a girlfriend I didn't know about."

"A girlfriend?" Trent let out a breath and she stole a glance at him.

"After that dance the girls from youth saw, was when I found out he had a girlfriend. I steered clear of him the rest of the party, but at the end of the night we ended up in what looked like an embrace.. The girl who invited me won't let me explain. She'd rather go telling lies about me and turning everyone at work against me."

Trent took a sip of his tea before replacing the mug on the counter. "Is she telling lies?"

His words hung between them a moment, drawing out the silence into awkwardness. As Hope wondered how to answer, she realized the question could be answered both ways to a degree.

"You've been blessed with confidence, Hope." Trent broke into her troubled thoughts. "Not to mention the ability to talk to anyone, anywhere, about anything. The enemy knows this. You put yourself on his ground, then he'll work things and play you to his plan. Which will never be for your good."

Hope slumped and balled her hands in her lap. Everything she did lately seemed to end up causing an issue, and she didn't know why. She was still the same.

Wasn't she?

Or was that the problem?

She reached for the cheesecake. As she pulled the plate back toward her, Trent's hand fell upon her own and she stilled.

Cheesecake was not the answer.

THIRTY

ope ambled into House and Home, watching her colleagues with a shrewder eye.

It felt like a veil had been lifted at work, and she could almost feel a stiffness in her colleagues as they greeted her. She even noticed the fake sudden distractions that just happened to take their attention as she was passing by. How had she missed this before?

Hope opened her locker to put her bag inside and headed out onto the floor. As usual, Rob had left her a note in the changeroom workbook with a list of jobs to get through before close of shift. Hope leaned on the bench and looked over the list with little interest when movement drew her attention. Liam and Rob entered the room mid-conversation. Hope straightened, plastering a welcoming smile on her face.

"Hope." Rob's dull eyes locked onto her. She hated how he looked at her and it took every bit of her willpower to keep a bright smile on her face and pleasing tone in her voice when speaking with him. "Good morning, Rob."

"There's a number of jobs backlogging that I've asked you to do. Make sure you make them a priority today, or I'll dock your pay."

Hope blinked and she felt her mouth drop open a moment before she snapped it back shut. He couldn't dock her pay! "Sorry, Rob, you're not allowed to dock my pay."

"Then I'll move your hours to be less accommodating to your extracurricular activities. I'm not paying you to stand around gossiping, deciding what you're going to buy next, or doing what someone else wants you to do rather than what I've asked you to do. Understood?"

Liam cleared his throat. Hope, unable to tear her eyes off Rob, caught him glance at her.

"Rob, Hope works hard while she's on the clock."

Rob turned to look at Liam, and Hope dropped her gaze. A hot, burning sensation filled her stomach as Rob's words played over in her mind. She didn't hear what he said to Liam, if he said anything. Everything had become white noise. As seconds ticked by, she became aware her eyes were beginning to sting. She knew what that meant. Without a second thought, she pushed past the men and hightailed it past the girls on the floor, and out the back.

Hands on hips, Hope drew in deep breaths to calm herself. It wasn't that Rob's words hurt, or she was so delicate she couldn't handle a rough word spoken to her. It was that she disliked him so much, the power he had over her tipped her over the edge.

A door shut behind her. She quickly wiped her eyes and shook out her hair.

"You ok?" Liam asked.

Hope huffed a breath out and turned, smile in place.

"Yeah, I'm fine." at least the lump in her throat had gone, so her words came out as if she really was fine. She had to get another job, and stat. Liam raised his eyebrows.

"I refuse to let him see how he gets to me. He makes me so mad. As if he can dock my pay. Does he think I'm that stupid?"

"Probably. He doesn't understand threatening staff doesn't result in better performance."

Hope rolled her eyes. "I knew he wouldn't notice I'd been putting in overtime. Why won't he just retire?"

Liam chuckled, took a pen from the back of his ear, and a notebook from his back pocket. "Well, I need to go through some old boxes out here, and I better not keep you from Rob's list of duties."

"Oh, please … don't." Hope held up a hand and went to step past Liam.

Then she remembered the girls out on the floor. She hadn't missed their expressions as she'd passed them in her hasty retreat. They'd be waiting for her to come back, feigning interest for gossip's sake. Knowing how they really felt about her now, she didn't want to talk to them anymore. She turned back to Liam.

"Actually, let me go through the boxes for you. I probably packed them anyway, so I'll sort it quicker than you." Hope reached for the notepad in Liam's hand, but he held it back from her and chuckled.

"No. You heard Rob."

"I'll get Rob's stuff done. I saw his list—it was just dusting and facing jobs. C'mon, gimme." Hope snapped her fingers and pointed to the notepad. Liam lowered his arm, and she plucked it out of his hand.

"You'd better. Rob doesn't just have a go at you, you know."

* * * *

Hope shone her pocket light over the boxes tucked away in the back of the storeroom to find the box Liam needed. Hope shoved a box aside, remembering the look on her colleagues' faces as she'd hurried past them, reminding her of the current state of play with the other girls, and reality as she knew it to be. They didn't care about her, just what happened to her.

"That you, Hope?"

Hope whirled around at the sound of Scott's voice, then caught herself with a breathy laugh. It was so quiet out the back, yet she hadn't heard him approach over the noise in her head. "Yeah, it's me. Just trying to find a box Liam is after. What are you looking for?"

Scott stopped beside Hope and distractedly cast his eye over the boxes surrounding them. "You."

Hope blinked. There was a seriousness in his expression, and she became aware of the narrow aisle she was working in.

She clicked off her pencil light and slipped it into her pocket, then lifted her shoulders. "Ok, you found me. What's up?"

"Is it just me, or are things a little frosty out there today?"

"A little? Try a lot."

"Any idea why?" Scott rested a hip against the shelving and crossed his arms. "When did you become the bottom of the heap?"

"Honestly, no idea. I only found out last week that my very presence is irritating, and the fact that you and I are out here talking will mean more daggers when I step back out onto the floor."

A lopsided grin crawled up Scott's face. "It annoys the girls that you talk to me?"

Hope let out a chuckle. "Not you in particular. More that I'm out the back talking to a guy at all."

Scott barked a laugh as he straightened. "Why?"

Hope laughed, not wanting to go through the story again. After all, it was her word against Claudia's and actions spoke louder than words—as Dave had been saying recently at youth. "It's a long, boring story. I'm sure you'll hear about it soon enough. Then you can decide if you believe it or not."

Scott's eyes narrowed on her as he appeared to think over what she'd just said. A smile began to curl on his mouth. "What if I like long, boring stories?"

""Both of us will get a long boring story from Rob if we don't get back to work."

Scott held up a hand and Hope high-fived him before he turned to leave. "Yes, I heard you've already had one lecture this morning. Be good."

Hope laughed as she clicked her light back on and continued searching for the box Liam was after. It was on the tip of her tongue to reply to Scott's comment with "aren't I always good?" but if she was, she wouldn't be in this situation.

Or would she?

THIRTY-ONE

Hope approached the steps of the homeless shelter the youth were serving at for their project and couldn't help the wrinkle that creased her nose. It looked like an old warehouse or youth hostel. All the windows were covered with beige blinds, and there was no garden to speak of. A single dull lantern illuminated the doorstep. It was quiet. Not even an evening bird sung.

Lexi was already inside, so Hope crossed the small verandah, took hold of the brushed silver door handle and entered. The boys would be arriving soon with the teens, so she needed to get to work helping Lexi set up.

After a short conversation with the receptionist, Hope hurried down the long corridor until she entered a large room, where Lexi was sorting something in the far corner.

"Hey, girl," Hope called out as she crossed the floor, hearing the slight echo of her words come back at her over the empty room. "What are you working on?"

Lexi hefted an arm full of blankets from a box onto the table beside her before brushing her fringe aside. "Boxes of donations. The receptionist asked if I could set it all out over this table for people to pick from tonight."

Hope picked up a luxe mink blanket and rubbed the cool velvety material against her cheek. "Why would someone give this away?"

Lexi chuckled and Hope lowered the blanket. "Seriously, they could have sold this."

"I'm sure whoever donated it knew how much it's worth, but they chose to give it away instead." Lexi took the blanket and refolded it, before pointing to another box. "Could you unpack that box for me, please? These items are gorgeous."

Hope set to work, admiring the pieces of clothing and household goods that had been donated, while thoughts about going to sleep, snuggled under that gorgeous blanket filled her mind. She definitely wouldn't have given it away. Maybe she'd have donated something from the back of the linen closet, or something out of style, at least. But how good would it feel to have that blanket wrapped around—

"Ok, everyone." Dave's voice broke into the stale atmosphere and Hope turned to greet him. The youths were fanning out from behind him and looking around the room.

"The kitchen is just behind where Lexi and Hope are working." Dave pointed as he spoke. "We need the bread buttered and soup heated ready to be dished up. The water dispensers need to be filled, and the muscles have just brought in boxes of pocket Bibles. These need to be put somewhere easy to reach, but not so obvious that they draw attention to anyone who may wish to take one. Let's get to work!"

"People should be arriving any minute." Trent appeared beside her. "Are you ready for an experience you'll never forget?"

Hope chuckled, her stomach feeling like a ball of wool. "Dave said this experience would be good for me, but I'm not sure what to expect."

"They're just people. People who've had 'life' happen." Trent turned away and joined Dave at the door to welcome those entering.

Surprised by how young those filing through the door were, Hope felt her insides twist uncomfortably. What could have happened to them for them to end up here on a Friday night? She swallowed. Something shifted within her.

"Hey, Hope. Could you give us a quick hand in the kitchen, please?"

Hope turned at Lexi's call and trotted to the kitchen.

Twenty minutes later, soups finished, and bread buttered, Hope was scrubbing dishes as Lexi pulled open the server window to show food was ready. The hall sounded a little like a library—quiet footsteps, muffled conversations, and the slight scrape of a chair being pulled out.

The mood felt somber. She wanted to step out into the hall and liven things up, to talk to people and perhaps even make them laugh. Surprised that she felt so drawn to this activity, Hope scrubbed a pot while thinking about how to get to know the people out there with the time they had, and how Dave linked this with her SHAPE results.

"Hey, girl, you're up for serving," Lexi called.

"Oh, Righto." Hope grabbed the tea towel next to her, and dried her hands, ready to see what she could do. Like Trent said, they were just people. She could handle people. With a flip of her wrist, she flopped the tea towel on the bench alongside her and looked up, ready to greet those at the servery window.

She stopped.

"Liam?"

Liam looked back at her, and his Adam's apple bobbed. "What are you doing here?"

Hope stepped up to the counter and cleared her throat. "I'm here with that youth group I told you about. We're volunteering here tonight. What are you doing here?"

Liam looked away as he ran a hand over his head. There was a grin on his face, but it wasn't a happy grin. Another person appeared at the servery. Hope handed them a cup of soup and held up the basket of bread, unable to take her eyes off Liam. He looked back at her and made a head gesture back into the room behind him, before he turned from the window and wove his way back into the room.

Hope watched him for a moment before hurrying back to Lexi at the sink. "Hey, Lex. Can I have … a ten-minute break?"

Lexi chuckled. "This isn't work, Hope. If you need to have a break, go for it."

Without a second word, Hope was out of the kitchen and weaving her way through the tables. She saw Liam and slipped into the seat opposite him. She tucked her hair behind her ears and clamped her hands between her knees as she leaned forward over the fold-out table. He would have to start this conversation.

"This is awkward." Liam's eyes still wouldn't find hers.

"Liam. you can look at me. It might make it easier to talk."

A wry grin curled on Liam's mouth a moment before his gaze locked on hers again. "I'm sure I know what you're thinking, and it's not that."

Hope stifled a laugh. She couldn't help it. The mix of pride and vulnerability from him just drew the response from her. "Ok. What is it then?"

Liam shook his head. "My story is similar to many others. Just keep that in mind."

"Which is?"

"Years ago, my family's business went bankrupt. We were in pretty deep. I had no idea. I was just a kid in high school. Anyway, we lost the house. I couch surfed with mates while my folks and sisters got accommodation at a caravan park in a borrowed caravan. I got a job as soon as I could, bought my own cheap van to get off my mates' couches. Long story short, I'm still there, saving every dollar I can so I can get myself through uni and eventually, buy my own place."

Hope felt her eyes widen. "That's a lot of information to get in one dump. Where does the homeless shelter fit in?"

Liam gave a smile and nod to someone in the room, then turned back to her. "We've come here for years. I would live on basically noodles and bread all week. This place gave me a good feed at least once a week."

Hope sat back in her chair and blew her breath out. "But your car ... your bike. I don't get it."

"I've had the dirt bike for years, and I refused to sell it. The car is borrowed. I tighten the belt until I can buy my own car. It is getting easier since I got the manager role at House and Home—that's how I was able to pay my membership to join The Valley Dirt Bike Club again. Now I can afford a few extra bits and pieces, I like to come back here as a volunteer and give back what I can."

Hope dropped her head. Her manicured nails caught her eye, and she balled her fists so she couldn't see them. First thing on Monday, she would cancel her ongoing monthly nail appointments. "Liam. If I only knew, or—"

"Or what?"

Hope looked up. The smile on Liam's face was not one of humor. "Help, I guess. In some way."

"C'mon, Hope. I hear you girls chatting about your next nail appointment and the parties coming up. I bet the homeless and less fortunate people all around us never crossed your mind until you came here."

Hope sat back in her chair. He was right. She'd read about homeless or seen them portrayed in movies but ... her thoughts cleared. An image reel of memories flicked through her mind of things she had read or watched. Things Nick and Dave had said echoed around her thoughts. Was it possible her whole perspective had been subtly altered? Suddenly, things weren't as rosy as she'd always thought. Before her was real. Around her was real.

A hand fell lightly upon Hope's shoulder, and she looked up to find Trent's serene expression focused on her. His words from earlier that evening came back into her mind, and a lump formed in her throat. Her mind was blown.

"It's time for us to get the youth back to the church for pickup."

"Right, yeah. Sorry, Trent. I lost track of time."

As Hope rose from her chair she turned back to Liam. So many things she wanted to say, to ask, but had no idea what they were. Liam stood and shook Trent's hand.

Though Hope watched the two men interacting, she was miles away in her head. She felt like her world had shifted.

What else wasn't what she thought it was?

THIRTY-TWO

The rays of the morning sun roused Hope, turning the blackness behind her eyelids to burnt orange and red. She yawned, rolled over, and rubbed her eyes. Her mind slowly cleared, and thoughts of the night before rolled in like a fog over the ocean.

Liam.

The heaviness in her gut resumed. With a flip of her hand, she threw her blankets back and sat up. What a night last night had been. Running a hand over her bed hair, Hope rose from the bed. As she crossed her room to the wardrobe to get dressed, she caught her reflection in the dressing table mirror—colored textured hair, pink silk pajamas, manicured nails. Her bedroom came into focus behind her. Queen-sized bed laden with pillows, heavy doona and chenille blanket, swag and tail curtains, plush carpets. She turned and looked at all she had.

She had so much.

What did she give back? Liam had hardly anything …

Hope blinked, wondering at the sudden thought that appeared in her mind. She ambled over to her window and looked out over the neighborhood bathed in the glow of the early morning sun. Liam was right. She'd never given a thought to others in her community. Why was that, and what was stopping her from starting? A fire began to ignite in her belly. It was different to other fires in the belly—first meetings, first dates, first kisses. First kisses were her favorite. This fire was different somehow. She thought about her SHAPE results.

Hope turned away from the window and went to her wardrobe to get dressed for church. Whatever was happening, whatever Dave was hinting her direction could be, she felt close to figuring it out.

As she reached for a beige asymmetrical skirt, her eyes fell upon her emerald-green Merino wool coat.

Donate it.

Withdrawing her hand from the skirt, Hope reached for the coat and ran her fingers over the soft material, wondering over the thought that had popped into her head. Something moved within her as she let her eyes wander over the exquisite coat. The chenille blanket came back to her mind, and she remembered her reaction.

Yesterday, not only would she never have thought of such a thing, but she would have thrown the thought out of her head the moment it entered. But now all she could think about was Liam and his family, about his remark—if she knew different, what would she do different?

Letting go of the coat, Hope picked a white V-neck long-sleeve blouse to pair with the skirt, then skipped downstairs for breakfast. Mum and Ryan were eating breakfast at the table. Mum waved her over. "Already got it ready for you, love."

With a grateful sigh, Hope sat and dug into the muesli and berries her mum had prepared for her when her phone beeped. It was Bec.

'Hey girl, you coming to watch the home game tomorrow? Not many left on the calendar now.'

The Valley Tigers were playing at their home ground tomorrow. They were edging towards the finals again. Josh was doing a great job since Dylan passed on the captain's job and it fell to him. It had been a while, and she would like to see him again. She spooned a mouthful of cereal into her mouth and hit reply.

'Sure. Meet you at the ground.'

* * * *

Hope stood next to her friends, listening to the final hymn, thinking about Liam again and wondering at the new feeling floating around inside her. It felt like excitement, but she wasn't sure what was causing the excitement. Was it the impression in her mind about donating the coat, or more? She chewed her lip.

God, help me put this puzzle together.

Once the minister and worship team had filed out, everyone took their seats, and Hope turned to her friends. "Anyone up for the football game tomorrow? Can't believe the season is almost over again."

Dylan laid an arm over the back of the church pew around Lexi. "A chance to watch Josh lead the Tigers to successive victories? Wouldn't miss it. Nick?"

"Got plans with Alice."

"You could bring her to the game?" Hope leaned across Lexi to emphasize her request.

Nick raised an eyebrow in return. "No."

Dylan shared a look with Nick as Lexi moved to get up. "C'mon, guys. Let's get to the hall for lunch."

The hall swelled with the sound of happy conversations and laughter as Hope made her way through the people towards an area to sit down in. Since an early spring storm blew in, luncheon had to be moved inside. It was cramped and loud, but still fun.

"You were deep in conversation with some bloke last night. Did you know him?"

Hope looked at Nick as she took a seat. He moved to sit opposite her in the horseshoe style layout the chairs were in. His voice held a note of restraint and his body seemed tense as he lowered himself into the white plastic chair.

"That's right. I was going to ask you about him on the way home, but I completely forgot." Lexi took the seat next to her. "He seemed familiar."

"Oh, him." Hope turned her attention back to Nick. "Yeah, that was Liam."

"Liam? The guy you work with?" Lexi gasped. Hope glanced back at her. Her eyes were like dish plates and her jaw had dropped open. Hope let her breath out with a chuckle. "Yep, that was him. He's got an incredible story. I can't stop thinking about it. It's going to be weird next time I see him at work."

Nick didn't often show he was surprised, but she had caught the flicker in those scrutinizing grey eyes. Satisfied, she looked over at Dylan. "How's your opinions of him now, boys?"

"Hope." Trent said, his voice quiet as he relaxed back into the chair and tucked his guitar beside him.

Nick coughed and cleared his throat, while Dylan made a study of his hands loosely clasped over his thighs.

Nick shook his head. "Well, I'm big enough to admit I've made a mistake. I ... ah ... judged the guy without reason." Nick looked back at Hope.

She reached across the space between them and patted his arm. "I know you did."

Dylan chuckled as Nick rolled his eyes. "I apologize too, Hope. He's been good to you, and we've been jerks about it."

"It's a good reminder that we don't know all of each other's stories." Trent's gaze swept the group. "The only thing we know for sure is that Jesus gave everything for us. If He sees such worth and value in someone, so should we."

Hope sat back in her seat and crossed her legs. "I just can't get past it. What are the odds of running into Liam? Of all the shelters in the city, Trent organized that one. Of all the days of the week we could have gone to serve, that's the day. Of all the times in the day we could have gone ..." Hope let the sentence hang.

"God has given you an insight into a colleague." Trent turned in his seat and rested an arm over the back of his chair. "What you do with that insight needs to be a prayer point."

Hope looked back at Trent and thought over what he said. What was God expecting of her? Liam knew she was a Christian, and she'd been able to witness to him a little. He seemed interested. She chewed a nail.

"Hope, stop thinking." Trent chuckled. "God is setting the pieces in place. You'll know when He wants you to move—if He wants you to move."

THIRTY-THREE

An icy wind whipped up Hope's hair as she walked towards the Valley Football Ground. She dropped her head against the breeze and hugged her red blazer closer. September weather was always unpredictable and made sitting beside an oval watching a game of football drag out. Why did she bother going?

To see Josh. Whether he wanted to see her or not.

The semifinal was upon them and Josh had had a great season so far. She hoped for him that the season would finish with a cup in hand. He deserved it. She also hoped they'd go to next week's vote count night together, but it looked like that wouldn't be happening.

"Hey, girl!"

Hope looked up against the wind and found Bec waving at her from just inside the gate. With stonewash jeans that could have been painted on and an equally tight ribbed black turtleneck paired with a white pom-pom beanie, she looked ready to party even in this horrible weather.

Hope embraced her. "You look amazing!"

"My wardrobe is yours, hun. Let's go, before we lose the good seats I saved."

Hope smiled as Bec took her hand and they hurried through the crowds. Clear ponchos and umbrellas were everywhere, and even the food vans had their lights on to stand out against the murky backdrop of the afternoon.

Surprised to find the ground side seats still free, Hope swung a leg over the wooden bench seat and sat as Bec dropped in beside her and handed her a poncho.

"Good. I was about to suggest heading back to the clubhouse. It's freezing out here in the wind."

"So what did you get up to for youth group last Friday night?" Bec wiggled into her poncho and readjusted herself on the hard seat as the teams ran out onto the field. They were beside the Tigers run.

"We went to a homeless shelter and helped out in the soup kitchen."

Memories came back of Friday night, and Hope found herself wondering what Liam might be doing. A laugh broke off her thoughts. She turned to see Bec beaming a great smile as she watched the players go through their warm-ups. Had Hope missed something? Bec chuckled again, and Hope turned back to her.

"What did I miss? What's funny?"

"You," Bec said through a laugh. "You, at a homeless shelter?"

Hope's stomach dropped to an uncomfortable weight in her gut as she looked back at Bec trying to reign in her amusement.

"You're serious?" Bec's smile fell away.

Hope looked away, then back at Bec. "Yeah. Why would I make that up?"

Bec shrugged. "I just can't imagine you visiting a homeless shelter. I'm sorry. I didn't mean to upset you. But I was imagining you serving at a homeless shelter, and it was a funny image." Bec's voice cracked and she chuckled again before covering her mouth with her hand.

Hope tried to keep a smile on her face as she turned her attention back to the game. Something was off within her. She couldn't stop thinking about Liam's story. How many other people around her right now were struggling or trying to claw their way out, like Liam?

"Hey." Bec's hand lay lightly on Hope's lap. "I upset you, didn't I?"

Hope shook her head and turned to look at her friend. "Oh, no. It surprised me but didn't upset me."

"You see the funny side, right?" Bec's voice dropped a note, and her smile faded.

Hope sighed. She had to be honest with herself—it was an amusing image. A homeless shelter was the last place anyone would expect to find Hope Meyer. "Maybe. Yeah, ok, I see it. But not anymore." Her voice trailed off and she looked back at the game.

"What happened?"

"Someone I knew was there." Hope glanced back at her friend. Bec's face had dropped.

After a slow blink she found her words. "Wow. Yeah, I can see how that would mess you up a bit."

Hope screwed her face up. "I'm not messed up. It just made me look at things differently—" Hope stopped herself and looked back at the game. Bec wouldn't be interested. She was just making small talk. Whatever Hope was feeling would be lost on Bec.

Who could she talk to about suddenly feeling a question mark over everything at the same time as feeling excited over something she couldn't explain? She straightened and drew in a deep breath through her nose. It was freezing. "I'm going to get a cuppa and something hot to eat. You want anything?"

Bec shook her head and pointed to a bag she was carrying. "I'm sorted thanks, hun. See you in a bit."

Hope meandered her way towards the food vans. What was wrong with her? A field full of eye candy, none more so than Josh, and she couldn't bring herself to enjoy the sight.

Or the company.

The warming scents of tomato relish and rosemary from the baked potato stand filled her nostrils. Hope stopped and looked over the menu. What was the most indulgent?

"Hey, you!" Lexi called.

Hope jumped and turned at Lexi's words. A weight lifted within Hope at the sight of her best friend, and she threw her arms around Lexi. The wind left Lexi's lungs with a laugh, and Hope laughed in return as she released her. "Sorry. Needed to … I don't know. I just needed a hug."

"And a big plate of greasies by the look." Lexi looked over the baked potato menu and the steaming food in the warmer, then back at Hope. "What's up?"

"What? I love baked potatoes."

Lexi crossed her arms and raised an eyebrow. Hope met her look and hoped the smile on her face would close the topic.

Lexi broke first. "How long have I known you? Football is over there, and you're staring at the baked potato toppings like you're usually staring at the players. Something's bothering you."

Hope laughed a little too loudly. "I'm hungry. Where are you guys sitting?"

Lexi eyed her for a moment longer before pointing to an area of the ground. "Dylan's just over there. Would you like to join us?"

Hope chuckled and shook her head, even though she would love nothing more than to shift camp. However, she had made plans with Bec.

Lexi eyed her a moment longer. "Alright then. Enjoy your greasies. See you Monday." Lexi headed back toward where Dylan was waiting.

Hope waved her friend off, then ordered a potato with the lot, plus extra toppings. She stood to the side and watched the game while waiting for her order, realizing that she didn't want to get back to the game—or was it the company she wanted to avoid? Hope dawdled by the cappuccino van, allowing others to go before her while she pretended to decide what to order.

Bec was making her uncomfortable. Her manner was grating, and Hope found herself recoiling at things Bec had implied. Was Hope that shallow? Was she really unempathetic and insensitive to others? She didn't think so. But she must be if that's what Bec and the girls at work thought.

Her SHAPE results came back to mind. She knew she was those things; Dave obviously knew it, her church family knew it too. So why did others see her differently?

With a frustrated growl, Hope stepped up to the coffee vendor and ordered her usual. She'd better get back to the game before Bec came looking for her. She did know one thing—she was close to figuring this out. Something told her it was all connected, that God was leading her somewhere, someplace. But where? To do what?

She needed to talk to Dave.

THIRTY-FOUR

"Hey, Hope, got a sec?" Liam asked in a hushed voice. Hope looked up from Rob's 'to do' list and found Liam standing just inside the changerooms, wringing his hands. She straightened and smiled even though her mind flashed back to the last time they saw each other, at the homeless shelter. The luxe mink blanket popped into her mind, along with her comments to Lexi. It was the warmest blanket among the pile of well-worn blankets. Did Liam have warm blankets in the caravan? Was he doing it tough? She forced herself to think of Liam as her supervisor, not someone who'd once needed the services of a homeless shelter while keeping a relaxed expression and moved around the bench to stand before him. "Yeah, of course. What's up?"

Liam cleared his throat. "First up, let me address the elephant in the room. I hope last Friday night doesn't change our working relationship."

Hope shook her head and tried to speak through her wild thoughts, but Liam held up a hand. "I'm sure that—"

"What happened last Friday night?" Claudia swanned into the room and dumped a pile of clothes on the workbench. Hope's mouth dropped open as Claudia turned suspicious eyes on her, then glanced at Liam.

Liam drew a in long breath. "Sorry, Claudia. Private conversation in process."

"Oh, I'm sorry. I'll come back later, once I've done the things that Rob's asked us to get finished this shift." Claudia reached over Hope, picked up the workbook and headed out of the change rooms. How many shots was that? Hope closed her eyes and drew in a slow calming breath before looking back at Liam. He looked over his shoulder then back at her.

"I just wanted to check you're ok. I can imagine what a shock it was … to see me—"

"No, no, it's all good." Hope took a step towards him. "If anything, I respect you all the more. You're inspiring."

"Thanks, Hope." Liam breathed a chuckle and rubbed the back of his neck, just as Jenny walked past the change room and looked pointedly at Hope. Hope grimaced inwardly but kept her smile upon Liam.

"Now that's out of the way, I wanted to ask if you could find a customer's order, since you know the stuff out the back so well." Liam's supervisor tone returned, and he was once again her superior. Hope tipped her chin up to him as she listened.

"Apparently, they ordered it a year or so ago, something came up and they never got around to coming in to collect it. As it's been so long, I couldn't assure them it was still out the back. Here are the details of the order. Can you head out the back and see if you can find it?"

"I'm on it." Hope plucked the slip of paper from Liam as she brushed past him and headed out of the change rooms.

"Hope."

Hope halted and turned.

"Thanks."

The simple word moved her, as it showed his vulnerable side again, the boyish face she hadn't known was hidden behind the hardened, almost bad boy look he had going on. His expression showed his genuine heartfelt gratitude because of something she had done. Albeit not much. But clearly it meant a lot to him. A lump formed in her throat as she smiled back at him.

"Anytime."

* * * *

Hope pulled up outside Dave's place early, eager to chat with him before the leadership team meeting and was thrilled to see she was first to arrive. Dave opened the door as she approached, and she skipped the last few paces to the entrance.

"Hey, Dave!"

"Come on in and have a seat."

Hope chuckled as she unhooked her bag from her shoulder and sank into a couch in the loungeroom. "I have one question, and then I think the puzzle pieces will fall into place."

Dave sat opposite her, hooking an ankle over his knee. "Fire away."

"Why did you think I'd enjoy the homeless shelter experience, but others think it's the funniest thing that I even set foot inside one?"

"Do you have your Bible with you?"

Hope nodded and pulled it out of her bag.

"Open up 1 Corinthians 15:33 and read it for me."

Silence fell over the loungeroom as Hope leafed through the wafer-thin pages of her Bible. Finding the page, she ran her nail down the lines until she found the verse he asked for.

"It reads. 'Do not be misled: Bad company corrupts good character.'"

Hope's smile fell away and she reread the verse to herself. Then reread it again. She looked up. Scratched an itch on her arm and breathed a laugh. "Um. Are you saying I'm one thing with you all and another thing with others?"

Dave sat forward. "Not exactly. I'm saying, people with your personality type tend to allow others to influence them, and that includes the things you watch or read. You have a big heart, Hope, and you don't like to say 'no' to people."

That was true.

"SHAPE revealed your spiritual gifts and heart, your abilities and personality. Combine this with your experience and you get an area of ministry God had shaped you specifically for. Every day is a ministry opportunity, and I see you making the most of those opportunities, but perhaps the reason you're not satisfied working as a sales assistant is because it's not exactly where God wants you."

"So where does God want me?"

"I've suspected the area you would thrive in for a while, and have been praying you'd discover it organically. However, while you appeared to lose your way, it seems God put the idea right under your nose through the suggestions box."

Hope tilted her head. "You think God wants me to work with homeless people?"

Dave handed her a business card. "Doesn't have to be the homeless. More general service for people in need. Give this lady a call and let God lead you from there."

Sounds of cars and a motorbike pulling up outside Dave's home filled the quiet that had settled over the room. Hope turned over the card in her hands. "Adventist Volunteers? Lexi has talked about these people."

"Yes. We're looking to have them host a youth night soon. But I'd like you to give Rose a call during the week." Dave said, as a knock sounded on the door.

Hope turned her eyes back to the Bible open in her hands and reread the verse Dave gave her. She couldn't deny when she went out with girls like Bec, she behaved in ways she'd never behave if she went out with Lexi. She just thought that was Lexi being more quiet; not as confident. But maybe it was her. Was she easily influenced, like Dave suggested?

"Hey you!" Lexi flopped into the couch next to her, and Hope flipped the Bible closed.

"Whatchya readin'?"

Before Hope could get into it, the boys all landed on the couches around them, and the room filled with chatter. Dave rejoined the group and called their meeting to start.

Hope struggled to keep her mind focused while the discussion about youth group circled around her. Her mind cleared the moment she heard 'dress-up' mentioned.

Dave was holding the suggestions jar the youth had filled with things they'd like to do, and the slip of paper Nick had pulled out. Hope smiled at the irony. He hated dressing up.

"C'mon, Nick. It's a bit of fun for the young people." Dylan stretched out on the couch and linked his hands behind his head. "You could come as some sort of centurion, like a police officer but back then?"

Hope smirked at the look Nick shot at Dylan. Nick couldn't laugh at himself. But then, in the wake of the detail he'd let slip to her the other night, how could he? It was serious stuff he dealt with on a daily basis.

"I think a dress-up will add another level of fun." Trent looked around the group. "Plus, it doubles as indirect teaching. Tell the youth it's a Bible character theme dress-up. they'll need to research their character to get ready."

"Well, I love it." Hope sat forward, already imagining who she'd come dressed as.

"You would."

Hope mocked Nick's glower across the room. "C'mon Nick. It'll be good for you."

Nick held her gaze and she softened her expression to a smile. He understood what she wasn't saying. Had he told the boys things he'd witnessed, or was he keeping things locked down under his steel-like demeanor?

"Ok, it's a 'come as a Bible character dress-up theme' this week." Dave's voice broke into her wonderings, and Hope snapped back to the conversation. He was making a note on his phone. "I'll message the youth. What's our icebreaker?"

"I think keep the evening activity simple, since the dress-up element will be in play." Lexi said. "Like … how about the photo perspective game? The one where you take close-up photos and others try to guess what the image is."

"I know the one." Dylan said, "Great idea."

"Yes, that is a great game!" Hope echoed.

Dave tapped a pen on his notepad. "Looks set, guys. Nick and Hope, you're on café duty this week. Lexi, Dylan, and Trent you're on set up and pack up. I'll leave it up to you all to decide who's taking the photos to use for the presentation. Also, let's not forget the upcoming beachside carnival. Have a think about who we could invite along and encourage the youth to think likewise. All good?"

Hope nodded her head and looked around the group.

This Friday night was going to be one of the best.

THIRTY-FIVE

ope grabbed her things and shut her locker with a loud clang.

And she'd started the shift in such a good mood too. Last night's brainstorming with the crew about the upcoming youth dress-up night and assigning each other characters to dress as had resulted in them laughing the evening away. As mad as she was, remembering it brought a smile back to her face.

But only for a moment. The girls at work seemed to be holding onto the gripe they had with her. She couldn't even raise a smile from them while playing practical jokes with Scott. He thought they were funny. As soon as she was home, she was going to call the number on the card Dave gave her last night and see where that might lead. Nothing was coming from her job search app profile, nothing in the paper grabbed her, and she wanted out of House and Home.

Drawing in a long breath of fresh air soon as she was outside, Hope strode towards her car. That was another thing about working indoors—the stale air. Maybe her next job could be an outside one.

"Where are you hurrying to? Church thing?"

Hope chuckled as Scott fell into step beside her. "Why? You wanna come along?"

Scott grinned, his gaze forward as they walked. "You have me curious. I can say that much."

"Curious?" Hope threw a surprised glance at Scott. "Why?"

"You're always so happy. There has to be something to it."

Hope felt her eyebrows jump at his assessment of her. She was a happy person—only some people seemed to be making it their goal to drag her down. "Well, bring that curiosity over one weekend and see for yourself." Hope paused at the busy intersection and waited to cross.

"I'm thinking about it. Yell out when you have your next social." There was a grin on Scott's face that Hope found encouraging.

"We're headed to the Beach carnival for youth social this month. You should come."

There was a break in the traffic and Hope stepped off the sidewalk and crossed the road. The basketball grand final was tonight, and she had to get home and get ready.

Scott lifted his arm in goodbye, called over his shoulder. "I'll think about it. See you next shift."

* * * *

Thankful to be home, Hope unloaded her coat and bag onto the coffee table and made her way through to the kitchen for a cuppa.

After setting the coffee machine, she scooped up the remote and switched on the living room TV to scroll Netflix for the latest recommendations. Selecting a rom-com she'd never heard of before, Hope collected her mug from the coffee machine and tucked herself up on the couch to relax.

However, her conscience did not let her relax.

She battled to focus on the storyline as Dave's words nagged at her conscience. *I believe you allow others to influence you, including the things you watch or read.*

Hope sipped her cuppa and pushed the thoughts from her mind. The handsome lead had just come back into the scene, heartbroken.

Ivory barked outside and Hope glanced towards the back door. She'd take Ivory for a run after the movie. This was her time to relax. With another sip of her drink, she watched the pretty heroine sit with the downcast hero and soon had him laughing. She smiled as she watched them chat and, watching the chemistry grow between the two left her feeling warm inside. As she watched, the two grew closer and closer, the conversation deepened, and they left the café together. With a wistful sigh Hope turned to look out the window. If only things could be like that in real life. So simple, so –

Hope caught herself. She sat up as she looked back at the TV. The lovebirds were taking a walk through a lamplit park. The melody playing in the background was uplifting and sweet, like springtime would sound like if springtime were music. Hope stood and watched the happy couple, her mind slipping the last piece of the puzzle into place.

How many times had she thought life would go this way, only to find nothing but heartache?

She had allowed herself to believe life was a romcom or a novel and she was the star. She had fashioned herself after fictional characters. No wonder her relationships never worked out. No wonder people thought she was a hypocrite.

Who was she when all the outside influences were removed?

Hope's heart pounded, and she turned from the couple's passionate embrace and snatched up the remote. A few clicks later, she had the settings panel up on Netflix, and deleted her profile from the family account. Then she tossed the remote into the couch, stormed out of the room, and headed to her bedroom.

You're supposed to be a Christian

Hope growled as Claudia's words came back to her. Hope was a Christian. She was. Her identity was in Jesus. He knew who she was.

Yet how could she be upset with Claudia when Hope hardly behaved like a Christian. An anger burst inside Hope as the big picture began to manifest out of the darkened areas of her mind. Now she understood why the girls at work disliked her, why Josh had distanced himself, why Nick mocked what she was putting in her mind, and why Lexi reminded her about stumbling blocks.

Her gripes toward them vanished as an uncomfortable tightness formed in her throat. She looked over her surroundings with clarity she'd never felt before.

It was time to remove everything inconsistent to who she wanted to be, starting with her wardrobe. She'd donate more than just that coat. She'd remove the pictures around her dressing table mirror and delete all the makeup influencer channels. Then, if she had time, she'd go through the bookcase.

First, she pulled out her phone to message Lexi and cancel going to the basketball grand final.

THIRTY-SIX

cool breeze whipped around Hope as she focused her camera phone on a corner brick of the church hall building. Touching her finger to the screen, she zoomed right in until each bump and crevice in the red stone filled her screen, then snapped the shot.

Lexi's laugh floated on the breeze somewhere on the church grounds. Hope turned to see Dylan reach a hand out to Lexi only for her to jump back, though she kept her phone pointed at him. Hope grinned. Of course Dylan wouldn't want Lexi taking a photo of him tonight.

She felt light of spirit since the big clean out. She'd taken a number of bags of clothes and shoes to the local op shop, where the volunteers were stunned by the condition of the items she'd dropped off. Hope grinned. She'd had to reassure the elderly ladies that she did want to give the items away, and the beautiful blessing they offered over her before she left. Her heart fluttered at the memory and her smile brightened all the more.

An ant on the footpath grabbed her attention, and she crouched down to take a close-up photo of it, just as a low rumble filled the late afternoon air. Nick was about to arrive. Hope chuckled. Had he dressed up as the character they'd assigned him?

"How many photos have you got?" Lexi's sang out across the open church lawns.

Hope captured the ant just before it hurried on its way again. "That's four."

The tip of something tapped her under the chin and she lifted her head. A plastic sword? Her gaze took in sandaled feet, a long white robe with gold belt, finished with a purple gown, to Nick's enigmatic gaze as he looked down at her. Hope raised an eyebrow, barely able to contain her grin.

"Rise." Nick's voice held a note deeper than usual. Hope raised her camera and snaped a picture before he could turn away.

"Delete that." Nick sheathed the plastic sword at his side.

Hope laughed as she rose to her feet. "Oh no, no! That is gold. It's one to show Miss Alice."

"Nick, you make a great King Jehu!" Lexi appeared beside Hope, phone in hand. "I love how much effort you guys put into tonight's costumes. Now I can't wait to see how Trent went getting his archangel costume!"

Nick harrumphed and readjusted the gold crown headpiece he was wearing. "Thanks, Lexi, but you two could have put more effort into yours."

Hope settled into a hip and gestured to herself. "And how do you think Hebrew midwives dressed?"

Lexi mirrored Hope's stance and Hope watched Nick's eyes dart between them. Dylan appeared, and Nick turned to him, raising an eyebrow. "Nice toga, brother."

Hope bit her lip as Lexi giggled. She had to admit, the moment she rocked up and saw all six foot five inches of Dylan wearing a toga, she'd burst into laughter. It took courage to wear that.

"How else do you think Ehud would have looked?"

Nick pointed to Dylan's hand. "And that's the sword your character reportedly used to kill King Eglon?" Nick's expression conveyed challenge and Dylan met Nick's gaze evenly.

"It's not a sword, King Jehu. It's a dagger."

Lexi elbowed Hope in the side and Hope looked at her. "Think they'll have a sword fight later?"

"I wouldn't put it past them." Hope chuckled at the image in her mind.

"Everyone looks the part." Trent's rich voice resonated from behind them, and Hope whirled around. Her breath rushed out at the sight of him. Sandals that laced up behind shin guards, a glistening silken white tunic overlaid with gold armor. Wrist guards snapped onto his muscular forearms, a shield in one hand and sword in the other, and a pair of wings rising up behind him.

"Wow!" The hairs on the back of Hope's neck rose as she gazed at him. "That is an angelic costume if I've ever seen one!"

"And the prize for best dressed goes to Trent." Lexi's eyes popped like Hope's. Did she wonder about Trent as well? Did she also think something was different? Hope looked back at Trent and found his gaze steady upon her.

"Impressive," Dylan said. "Where did you score a costume like that?"

Trent sheathed the glinting sword behind him and looked at Dylan. "It's just something I had lying around."

A gasp from Lexi drew Hope's attention back to her. She laid a hand on her friend's arm. "What?"

"Hope, we have to finish taking the photos for tonight's ice-breaker." Lexi's words were rushed as she fumbled her phone to get the camera app open again. "Guys, we'll catch you in the hall shortly. Can you make sure the projector and cables are set up for us, please?"

Dylan nodded and headed towards the hall with Nick and Trent in tow. Hope watched the boys depart for a moment before taking off after Lexi. Now wasn't the time to ask Lexi what she thought about Trent.

Twenty minutes later, Hope had just finished putting the finishing touches on the presentation when the first of the dressed-up youths made their way into the hall. Excited chatter and laughter over the array of costumes on display filled the room. She noticed a new face in the crowd. The look of unease was obvious on the young man's face at being the only one not in a costume. Hope hurried over to him only to reach him at the same time as Trent.

They locked eyes. Hope stepped back with a sweeping motion for him to take the lead.

"Welcome to the Valley Youth Group. I'm Trent, this is Hope, and we were just admiring your costume." Trent held out his hand.

Hope's eyes darted from the nervous young man to Trent, and back again, wondering where he was going with that. "What's your name buddy?"

"Blake." Blake shook Trent's hand. "Ah, what costume? My mates who invited me didn't tell me it was a dress-up night or something. Think I'll head off. I'm feeling pretty uncomfortable. Nice to meet you both."

Blake turned to leave. Hope's mind whirled. Was there anything she could to find him among the backstage dress-up wardrobe and props? Trent chuckled. She tilted her head.

Trent had his hands on his hips and a cheeky expression on his face. "Wait. You're not in costume? Hope and I were discussing how clever it was for you to come as an angel dressed in common clothing."

A grin curled on Hope's face. She was about to pick up where Trent left off when a number of the teens pounced on Blake from behind, knocking him forward. Hope jumped back as the boys roughhoused. After some hurried hello's, they all disappeared into the hall. Hope blew her breath out as Trent came to stand beside her.

"Good pick up. Thanks Hope."

"Thank me? Thank you. That was a great cover. I never would have thought of that."

Trent looked over the room. "Yet it's true. Angels do get around, dressed just like us." He turned to look at her. "Well, except for tonight."

Hope's stomach bottomed out and a sprinkle of goosebumps wove up her arms. Did he just confirm what her intuition had been trying to tell her? Eyes narrowed, she watched Trent move back into the room full of teens. He never paused for long with an individual, just long enough to draw a smile from them. What did he say? What encouragement did he give? She had to talk to him. This question in her mind was starting to drive her nuts.

Hope was about to follow him when Dave stood to welcome everyone to youth group. Remembering her role for the night, she hurried back to the projector. That chat with Trent would have to wait for another time.

After a short introduction, the youth took their seats on the beanbags, pillows, chairs, and couches strewn around the hall and fixed their eyes on the big projector screen. When Dave gave her a nod, Hope flipped up the first close-up photo on the list. She beamed as the hall filled with shouts and laughter-filled suggestions of what each image was.

A thought sprung to mind. Stifling a giggle, Hope snuck in the image she'd taken of Nick, and the room roared with laughter. Dave gave Hope a keep-it-moving motion with his hand, and she flipped to the next close-up image. She could feel Nick's eyes boring into her from somewhere in the room, and her smile widened all the more.

When the time on the last picture elapsed and the youth had submitted their guesses as to what the image was, Dave indicated for Hope to start the slide show again, so that each picture could be seen from its zoomed-out perspective.

After the youth discussed the last of the photos, Dave paused a moment and looked over the now-quiet hall.

"A lot of us are looking at life like the first camera roll—up close. We get lost in the day-to-day humdrum of life, and—more often than not—we're looking short-term and our focus is on ourselves. So we look at life and we're confused. But, in the same way the confusion fell away when you saw the zoomed-out pictures, so the confusion of life falls away when you turn your attention to Jesus. Jesus helps us see the bigger picture and what role each of us have to play. Your priorities will shift. I challenge each and every one of you to pull your focus back a notch. Ask Jesus to show you the big picture and your role in that picture."

At Dave's cue, Hope put music on and started packing away the projector while those around her packed up the hall to get ready for games afterwards. Then she headed to the kitchen.

As soon as the doors closed behind her, Hope set herself to task cutting up the fruit platter for supper while thinking over what Dave had said. That realization of looking at things too closely had hit her just the other day. It blew her mind.

"You're quiet tonight."

Hope looked up. "I didn't even hear you come in."

The corner of Nick's mouth hitched as he leaned back against the serving counter. "I noticed. I also noticed that you're cutting up fruit. What's on your mind?"

"Just thinking about what Dave said." Hope put down the knife and leaned on the counter. She wasn't even sure how to put all the thoughts in her head into words. "I realized the other day that my perspective is probably different to most other people's."

Nick chuckled as he reached for a handful of grapes.

"Nick, I'm serious.

"What did you expect? You can't spend as much time as you do watching chick movies focused on a small moment of time, and think the fantasies won't affect you in some way. We spoke about this at my place on Sunday night."

Hope shook her head and blew out a long breath. "I know, and thank you for having the guts to tell me. I guess what hit me the other day was that I'm not sure who I am. I mean, I know my identity is in Jesus, but I don't know what that means, what it looks like. Does that make sense?"

Nick threw back the rest of the grapes in his hand, then stooped to get the mugs out of the cupboard under the island bench. "You know, there is some statistic about how the average person spends three hours a day watching tv or other type of media, and only thirty minutes in Bible study."

Hope picked up the knife and continued chopping the fruit. "What's that got to do with what I just said?"

"The Bible tells us by beholding we become changed. So switch it up, Hope. Pick up your Bible."

THIRTY-SEVEN

"Fruit salad? Not profiteroles?"

Hope shared a laugh with the mobile food van attendant. She knew the woman, and often had a good conversation with her on Sunday morning market days, so she took the comment in good humor. "That's right, no profiteroles today. I'm trying to make better food choices, and that fruit salad looks fabulous!"

Still smiling, Hope raised the fruit-laden fork to her mouth and turned to head back into the crowds. It was a beautiful early spring day and the local market was in full swing.

A smile on her face, she ambled through the market, looking at the different stalls, wondering about God's hand over her life. Nick had told her to pick up the Bible instead of a book, so she had. She'd let the Bible fall open, and the first thing she'd read was a text about being God's handiwork, created in Jesus to do good works, which God prepared in advance for us to do. All she had to do was find what those good works were … and she had a strong sense that had something to do with Adventist Volunteers.

She wanted to phone them, so Monday morning couldn't come quick enough. She had already followed their social media pages and watched a number of promotional videos and couldn't stop thinking about it. God's timing was perfect. Now she'd cleaned out her room and taken the bags to the op shop, she was even more ready to talk to whoever answered her call tomorrow. She popped another piece of fruit in her mouth.

"Hope?" a kind male voice said from beside her.

"Oh! Hi, Josh. Wow, seems like a long time since I've seen you." She spoke into her hand, hoping food wasn't stuck in her teeth.

"Likewise." His eyes held an inquisitive gleam as if he was seeing her for the first time, and she was sure one of his eyebrows twitched. A grin began to tickle the corners of her mouth as she watched his gaze sweep over her. He smiled. "What have you done different?"

Hope held out the sides of her flowing maxi skirt and looked over herself—pink casual shirt tucked into a floral maxi skirt with a weave belt for detail and white ballet flats peeking out underneath—then looked back at Josh. "What do you mean?"

His smile sent her heart up a notch. "It's just … Well … you look, like you're … glowing. And you're not wearing any make-up."

Hope glanced away as she tucked a piece of flyaway hair behind her ear and readjusted the sunglasses on her head. How did Josh see glowing? What did he mean?

"This is me now. Flaws and all. Overhauled my wardrobe and threw out my make-up, except for one tub of pawpaw. What girl is without a tub of pawpaw, right?" Hope knew she was babbling, but her mouth was suddenly dry, and she felt … vulnerable. She'd only just changed how she presented herself and was still getting used to her new look. She hadn't expected to run into Josh.

Josh pocketed a hand as he gestured over her with the other. "What flaws? You've always been beautiful. Only now I feel like I can actually see you. I'm not trying to see you through a mask or something. Anyway, there's a glow about you that's different. It's in those eyes …" He drew in a long breath and gave a dreamlike smile as he plunged his other hand into his jean pockets. Hope looked down as she scuffed a bit of sandy path with her shoe. This was crazy. It felt like a first meeting.

Josh let his breath out on a soft chuckle, then cleared his throat. "So … meeting anyone here today?"

Hope shook her head and looked back up at him. "Just me."

"Don't often see you with a bowl of fruit salad in hand."

Hope matched Josh's cheeky grin and tipped her chin. "Like I said, I've been making some changes lately."

"I can see …"

An awkward silence dropped over them. Hope glanced around the market and wondered how she could either keep the conversation going or, end the conversation and leave?

Josh cleared his throat again. "You got time for a chat?" Josh motioned towards an empty café table nearby. A light breeze stirred up the sandy path beneath her feet and enveloped her in the woody masculinity scent of his cologne.

Hope looked at the table, then back to Josh, part nervous and part stirred by his gentle invitation after how she'd treated him. She nodded her head and moved towards the table. She couldn't believe the butterflies in her stomach as Josh settled himself opposite her. She felt like she had on their first date.

"How have you been?"

Josh chuckled. "We're not done talking about you yet. I'd like to hear what's been happening with you."

A number of possible answers came to mind, but she couldn't move past the need to the bypass small talk and hit the issue between them.

"Josh, I need to say straight up how sorry I am for how I treated you when we were together. I'm not apologizing because I'm looking for a second chance or anything. I just need you to know I understand why you stepped back and thank you. If you hadn't done that, I don't know where I'd be right now."

Hope dropped her head as memory after memory stormed her mind and her insides felt heavy with guilt. Seeing him was so unexpected, but it had cemented a distant thought in her mind that wouldn't go away. She loved him. She did. But she couldn't undo what she'd done or things she'd said. All she could do is think more of others and keep her perspective zoomed out—

"Hope?"

Hope looked up. Josh clasped his hands over the small café ironwork table between them. "Hey. It's ok. It's more important to me how you are."

"I'm doing really well."

"Good."

"Are you ready for the Grand Final this weekend?"

Josh's eyebrows jumped as he sat back in the chair. "I'd like to think so. You going to come along? It was good to see you on the boundary line the other week."

Hope's heart skipped a beat. He had seen her there with Bec. Thoughts came to mind to playfully counter his question, but instead she battled her mind for something real.

What was real?

How she felt. No games.

"Of course. Nowhere I'd rather be than seeing you lead the Tigers to win back-to-back premierships."

Josh's laugh filled her soul with warmth, and she met his gaze with a smile she couldn't contain.

"If we're going back-to-back, I'll need my lucky charm watching."

THIRTY-EIGHT

ope was dreading work on Monday. She knew her days at House and Home were drawing to a close, and she could deal with the status quo while there was no clear end in sight. But since her morning phone conversation with Rose from Adventist Volunteers, all she wanted to do was resign, explore the exciting opportunities they had listed on their website, and apply for one. Hope grinned as she walked; unbelieving the path she was looking at going down. Hope ... a professional volunteer? Oh, some people would laugh. But surprisingly, she didn't care.

The store was quiet as everyone was still setting up for the day. As she approached the changerooms, Hope heard a male voice speaking with Claudia. She paused outside to listen.

"C'mon, Clauds. Why not?"

That male voice sounded familiar. Hope leaned closer to try and identify the muffled voices.

"Why not? Because I don't think it's a good idea."

"You can think that all you like," the male voice said. "You won't change my mind. I'll run into her sooner or later."

Hope fussed with some nearby clothing racks so she could eavesdrop but look like she was working. Who was that and why did Claudia sound so annoyed? Who did this person want to run into?

"Morning, Hope."

Hope whirled around at Liam's greeting just as the conversation ceased in the changeroom behind her.

"Have a good weekend?"

"Yes. Yes, it was great. Yours?" Hope flicked a glance towards the changerooms, expecting Claudia to poke her head out any minute.

Liam referenced the tablet in his hand. "We've just had a delivery of summer stock. Can you and Claudia begin setting up a summer stand and putting aside potential markdowns for the October sale?"

Claudia exited the change rooms with Rowan trailing behind. Hope couldn't help her mouth drop open. What was he doing here? He was the last person she ever wanted to see again.

Liam looked up. "Ok, Hope? Can I leave you with this?"

Hope caught Rowan look over at her and she turned back to Liam. "Yeah, yeah. No worries at all. I'll get on it right now."

A hushed conversation broke out between Claudia and Rowan. Liam looked over at them, then back at Hope. "Right then. I'll leave you to your customer."

"No." Hope took a step out from the clothing racks to pass behind Liam. "Claudia's got this. I'll get started on the display."

"Hi, Hope." Rowan took a step towards her, and Claudia turned with a huff back to the changerooms.

Tight-lipped, Hope turned to Rowan. "Hi."

She glanced in Liam's direction, wishing Rowan would just go away.

As if reading the situation, Liam pointedly looked at his watch. "Rob will be out shortly." He turned away.

Liam had just given her the perfect out. A grin threatened to emerge, but she pushed it down and turned back to Rowan. "What's up?"

"I've been hoping to run into you, but never seem to catch you." Rowan stepped closer, and Hope stepped back and pretended to straighten some clothes.

"Ok. Why?"

"I'd like to ask you out. Are you free for lunch? Today, maybe?"

Claudia stormed from the changerooms, her arms loaded with clothes and an expression that could kill. Hope's heart thumped. "Sorry, Rowan, I'm not interested."

His mouth curled into a smile that turned her stomach, and he leaned towards her, resting an elbow on the clothing rack she was straightening. "Didn't seem that way when we were dancing ..."

Hope turned to face him. He seemed so confident she'd say yes that the fact she'd said no hadn't registered. "Maybe not right at that moment. Then I found out you had a girlfriend with you that same night. I'm not interested in dating guys like that. So thank you for the offer but it's a no. Now I need to get back to work."

Hope moved around him to head out the back before he could answer, but not before she caught the subtle darkening of his countenance. She hadn't gone five steps before she heard his sniff of derision. "Claudia was right. You are just a tease."

Hope whirled around to see him stalk off.

Unable to put a thought together, she glared after him until he disappeared. Claudia said that? And he had agreed? She felt sick.

Just then, Claudia came back into her view and went into the changerooms. Anger bubbled within Hope and she stormed after the girl.

"How does Rowan know I work here?" Hope tried to keep her tone light, but she could feel the pressure building within her chest. Claudia looked up from the workbench full of clothes she was sorting. "He asked, and I told him."

"And was that when you told him I'm a tease?"

Claudia looked up, and her face boomed with color. She appeared to compose herself, and Hope thought for a moment that Claudia was about to retract her unfair comments and apologize.

"You have a problem with people telling the truth?" Claudia chuckled as if she'd made a joke. "Of course you would. You call yourself a Christian."

Hope blinked. The intensity coming from Claudia must have been building up, but it was misplaced. "Whoa, whoa, whoa. That's going a bit far."

"Really? Because from where I was that night, it looked like you two needed to get a room." Claudia moved out of the room with clothes to re-hang. She was trying to avoid the conversation, but Hope wasn't going to wait until their break to sort out whatever was going on. She took the opposite side of the clothing rack and worked the same. Careful to keep her voice down, she angled towards Claudia.

"I've told you what happened. I'm telling the truth. Why don't you believe me?"

Claudia raised her eyes and glared at Hope over the rack of clothes, her voice hushed but full of spite. "That is not his version of the story."

Hope bristled. "What's he saying?"

"He says he was just trying to get past you, and you grabbed hold of him and bent yourself backwards so far, he tried to stop you from falling. He's been obsessing about you since because of how much you apparently want him, so he broke up with his girlfriend for you and came to ask you out. Then, if I heard right, you rejected him." Claudia moved to another clothing rack. "And you wonder why you're described as a tease?"

Hope swallowed past the bile in her throat, knowing that story was circulating about her. She glared at her work colleague. "Don't tell me you actually believe that? You know me better than that."

Claudia moved away again and headed for the adjacent shoe racks. "I was surprised to see you dance like that in the first place, but I don't know why. I've seen you and Scott dance like that at staff functions. I don't know what to believe."

Dumbfounded, Hope watched her colleague, unsure of what to say next.

Stay on topic. Rowan came onto her.

She marched over to Claudia. "Then look at the evidence. Who came up to who on the dance floor? Who moved in to kiss who? Who didn't tell who they were taken?"

Claudia stood after retrieving shoes from the floor and looked about to interrupt, when she fell silent and turned back to the shoe shelves next to her. Hope fell silent as the hairs on the back of her neck stood on end, moments before she heard the dreaded voice.

"Girls. My office. Now."

THIRTY-NINE

ob's office was as dreary as the man who occupied it. Four grey walls with only a corkboard holding Health and Safety notices and payroll checklists gave something to look at. The work desk held minimal items, all stationery. Did the man have a loved one? There was a subtle body odor smell about the room and Hope curled up her nose just as the door behind her was shut.

Rob made his way past her and sat. He remained quiet, looking at some notes on his desk. Hope shot a glance at Claudia, who was looking straight ahead, a vacant and unimpressed look upon her face.

"Ladies, do you know why I've called you into my office?"

Hope mentally rolled her eyes and remained silent. Claudia cleared her throat. "I'm sorry, Rob."

"Hope?" Rob prompted. Hope turned her eyes to him. "Something to add?"

When she remained silent, Rob exhaled loudly. "I've called you both in because I could hear your little argument. I don't care what it was about, but what have I told you about leaving your private lives at home?"

Hope cleared her throat. "I'm sorry, Rob. I was trying to sort out someone telling lies about me."

Claudia shot her a look, but Hope kept her gaze forward. "Well, Hope," Rob said. "That conversation can wait until your shift has finished—"

"So you're judging people now? Nice."

Hope shot Claudia a look. "I'm not judging anybody. What's with you lately?"

"Girls." Robs voice was low and ominous, like distant rolling thunder. Hope ignored him and kept her questioning gaze on Claudia.

Claudia glared back at her. "Nothing's with me. I am what you see—unlike *some* people."

"Girls, anymore out of either of you and I'll dock your pay." Rob folded his arms across his chest.

Hope's heart began to pound and she squared herself to Claudia. "Excuse me?"

Claudia's eyes flashed as she looked back at her just as Rob stood behind his desk. "Well, I'm not the one masquerading as a youth group leader while out partying on weekends, flirting with every man I come across, and coming onto other girls' boyfriends—"

"Right, both of you, docked pays."

"—I thought you were a Christian."

Hope gaped at Claudia, who turned on her heel and marched out of Rob's office. The door slammed behind her, and Hope jumped. She stared at the closed door until Rob cleared his throat and she turned back to him.

"You're on an official warning, Hope. Claudia is too, but I'll catch up with her later. You'll receive a letter outlining why this has been issued. If I have to deal with this again, you'll find yourself looking for another job."

Hope heard Rob's words, but they were barely audible in her mind under Claudia's accusation. *I thought you were a Christian.*

The charge echoed over and over until Rob thumped his desk, and Hope's mind cleared. She looked at him and encountered that look that dripped with everything that was detestable in life.

"Are you listening to me, Miss Meyer?"

Hope's jaw clenched. He would not make her cry. Not again. She was done with his black presence hovering over her life, his threats, and his uncaring nature. It rubbed against everything she was. Her heart thumped, her breaths coming short and fast. She stepped up to his desk. "I quit. Effective immediately. And I'll be reporting you to HR for threatening to dock my pay."

Hope turned and left his office. Rob's door closing behind her silencing his parting remarks. She headed for the staff room, collected her things, ripped off her name badge, and binned it at the front entrance as she strode out of House and Home for the last time. Her eyes burned with the tears she was fighting to keep back, Claudia's charge shouting in her mind.

Hope wiped her eyes as she walked. She was a Christian. She was a Christian!

The Bridgeshore Plaza sliding doors opened as she approached, and she broke into a brisk walk once out in the fresh air. Images filled her mind from many weekends past and conversations had, what others must think of her, the lies that Rowan was repeating.

Claudia was right. You're just a tease.

Hope hurried towards her car, just wanting to get home. Fumbling her keys, she couldn't shake Claudia's words from playing over and over.

I thought you were a Christian.

A crushing sensation filled her body and she slumped into the car seat moments before dissolving into tears. What was she going to do now? She had quit her job and had nothing lined up except a meeting with the volunteer agency. How could the clouds be clearing and finally getting a sense of direction, then it be snatched away through misunderstandings and flat-out lies?

Hope drew in a ragged breath and started her car. The tears dried up and anger started to pool in her gut. She pulled out into the traffic and headed for home. What on earth did she do to deserve this?

All of a sudden, her mind recalled her conversation with Lexi at the beachside market and Lexi's gentle warning.

Beware the struggles that will come when you try to make positive changes.

FORTY

ope stepped inside her family home and leaned back against the door until it clicked closed.

She'd cried and screamed herself out all the way home, and now she felt numb. She needed a coffee, and she was sure she had seen a pack of Tim Tams in the back of the cupboard.

Beware the struggles that will come when you try to make positive changes …

Hope sighed as she rolled her eyes. Fine. A glass of water and some fruit.

Hope pushed away from the door and made her way through to the kitchen. She flipped her bag onto the kitchen bench, then leaned over the bench and tried to reign in her rolling emotions. Mid-breath, her phone rang and she scrambled through her bag to find her phone. There. And Josh's name was on the screen. She scooped up the phone, cradling it in her hand like it was a lifeline, and answered the call.

"Hey, Hope. What's happening?"

The sound of his voice was like a soothing balm inside her mind. She took a deep breath and released it before responding. Her chest hurt from the strain. "Oh, I'm alright. You?"

A light chuckle came down the line and she imagined him outside his place, one hand in his pocket, the other holding the phone, looking down as he scuffed a boot along his gravel driveway.

"I have the day off today, so I went to your work to see if you wanted to grab a bite in your lunch break, and I was told you quit. So … what's happening?"

Hope covered her mouth. He had come to see if she wanted to have lunch. Unbidden, her eyes filled, and a lump formed in her throat.

"Hope? You there?"

"Yeah. Yeah, I'm here. I'm just … so happy you called." Hope knew her voice sounded too rushed and pitchy. He'd see right through it.

The deep sound of Josh clearing his throat came through the line and Hope bit her lip. This was where she was in a constant state of confusion. Were they together or just friends? The line was hard to see, and his pause told her he struggled with this too.

"Would you like me to come around?"

Hope gripped the phone. *Yes! Yes, I would love that!* She closed her eyes. "I'll be ok. Don't put yourself out. It was something I had to do, and it was a long time coming."

"I'll see you in ten."

The line went dead. Hope opened her eyes and looked at her phone. Her heart geared up a notch. Josh was coming over. The last time he'd come over, he'd ended things. Hope looked around the empty kitchen and living area, tucked in her shirt then smoothed out her skirt, and swallowed hard.

Almost exactly ten minutes later, the doorbell rang. Her heart fluttered as she walked to the door while her mind ran a mile a minute with thoughts tumbling over one another. She took a deep breath, blew it out, and opened the door with a beaming smile. "Hello, you!"

Josh's smile was as warm as the sun after a rain and more than reached his eyes. He dipped his head. "Well, that's not the face I was expecting. You look great."

Hope stepped back and gestured for him to enter. She took a deep breath of his cologne as he passed, and couldn't help but smile as she closed the door. That was the one she'd once told him was her favorite.

Josh relaxed into the lounge suite. "So what's happening? Why did you really quit?"

Hope took an adjacent seat, slumped over her arms, her chin resting in her palm. "Well, long story short, Rob threatened me again, so I quit and walked out. Just like that. I can't stand bullies."

Hope took in Josh's pensive expression. She'd left a few details out, and hoped he wouldn't ask her if that was all.

Josh's features darkened. "He threatened you?"

A thrill ran up Hope's spine at the uncharacteristic growl in Josh's voice. "Threatened to dock my pay."

"He can't do that."

"I know. I told him I was reporting him to HR." Hope flashed a smiled to reassure him all was well. The tightness in his features and fire behind his eyes when she said that Rob had threatened her calmed her spirit. He still had feelings for her.

"Good." Josh readjusted himself on the couch. "So what's your plan now?"

Hope inched forward on the couch, angling herself towards him. She'd wanted to tell him what was happening yesterday at the market, but for some reason it didn't feel like the right time. But now, in the quiet of the sun-bathed loungeroom, she wanted to let him in.

Conversation flowed easily, like old times, until well into the evening. Hope's family greeted Josh when they came home, then retired to the kitchen and living area to give them privacy. "I hope I'm not boring you with my waffle, as Dad would put it." Hope lightly brushed Josh's knee. A handful of lamps filled the room with a warm glow after the sun slipped below the horizon.

Josh gave a light shake of his head, his eyes aglow from the lamp light next to him. "No."

"Really?" Hope tried to rein in her smile. His opinion of her meant more than she had thought. Realizing how her actions impacted people around her had been a bitter pill to swallow, though she loathed herself most for hurting the man in front of her.

He moved himself forward on the lounge, mirroring her posture. "I knew there was something different about you when I saw you yesterday. You're happier—if that's possible."

Hope chuckled, dropping her head a moment before looking back at him.

"You seem more grounded. You have a plan, a direction, and from what I see and hear this afternoon, your faith is more real to you now." His hand found hers, his fingers entwining around hers. Hope drew a breath through parted lips, lost in the liquidity of his brown eyes, relishing the warmth spreading throughout her body. "I have loved being here this afternoon with you, but I need to get going."

Hope gave a slow nod as he dropped his gaze. Her breath caught as he raised her hand to his mouth and brushed his lips over the back of her hand. Drawn to the tender gesture, Hope watched as he lingered, the touch of his mouth on her skin again filled her with a longing to be his once again.

Maybe, someday soon, they'd find their way back to each other. She missed him so much.

FORTY-ONE

dreamy smile lit Hope's face as she ate a leisurely breakfast. Last night with Josh had even featured in a dream she had—only the night ended a little differently. Hope grinned into her bowl of muesli. She couldn't wait to see him again.

Her phone buzzed, and she drew it to her. She hadn't looked at it since taking the call from Josh yesterday.

She gasped. Three missed calls and five messages. She'd just received a new message from Lexi. Leadership was last night. She had totally forgotten! She typed a message back to Lexi.

'Hey, I am so sorry I missed last night. Had a rotten day, then Josh called by, and I forgot all about leadership meeting. I'm free all day today. Could I pop by for a catch up?'

Hope sank back in the chair, checking her other messages while she waited for a reply. Two calls from Lexi and one from Dave. One tongue-in-cheek message from Nick, another call from Dave and two more from Lexi. Hope sighed just as her phone beeped again and she opened the message.

'So good to hear from you! We were all so worried. Yes, I'm home from one today. Pop round. Lex.'

Still feeling awful about being a no-show last night, Hope shoveled down her breakfast. She'd find a way to make it up to the team. Maybe she could pull double duties to give the others a night off to relax with the youth?

Once breakfast was done, Hope meandered upstairs to shower before heading over to Lexi's.

* * * *

Dylan's Harley and Shaun's work ute were both in the driveway when Hope pulled up out the front of Lexi's place. She frowned. She thought she had Lexi to herself this afternoon.

The door was open. Hope would normally just walk in, so she did again. As she made her way down the hallway, soft voices and intermittent laughter came from the kitchen. She stepped quietly into the open-plan living area and saw Lexi and Dylan in the kitchen. The bench behind Lexi was littered with cups, the milk was out and the kettle bubbling. Dylan moved towards Lexi and embraced her, saying something too quiet for Hope to hear before they shared a soft, lingering kiss.

Hope looked away. Last night came to mind and how much she'd wanted Josh to kiss her. She breathed a soft sigh. Surely the kiss on the hand as he left was a positive sign that they'd get back together soon.

The sliding doors opened, and Shaun walked in from the garden. "Hey, hey, hey, you two. Enough of that in my household." His smile was playful, and Dylan turned to him with a droll look.

"Yeah, righto, Dad!" Lexi joked back to her brother, just as Shaun locked eyes with Hope across the room.

"G'day Hope."

Lexi turned to her at Shaun's greeting and chuckled. "Oh, Hope. I didn't hear you come in. Wanna cuppa?

Hope shook her head as Shaun collected his wallet and keys off the counter. He was leaving. With great poise Hope pushed down the awkwardness curling in her gut from busting her best friend in a private moment, and from seeing Shaun while she wasn't wearing any makeup.

"You ok? Aren't you normally at work about now?" Lexi glanced at Hope as she began to fill the cups on the bench with hot water. "You look pale."

Hope pulled a laugh from somewhere within herself and perched on a bench seat, trying to ignore the scrutinizing gazes coming from the boys. "Oh, yeah, I'm good."

Lexi offered Dylan a mug. Just before he took a sip, he lowered it. "You're not wearing any makeup. That's what's different about you."

Hope nodded, aware a blush was filling her cheeks. At least she wasn't pale anymore. "Nope. This is me, as God made me. Trying to learn to love it, instead of altering it."

An awkward silence fell over the room and Hope met all their eyes with a smile. If only they knew how much her gut was churning right now. Shaun cleared his throat, and a warmth lit his features as he looked back at her. "You never needed it anyway."

Hope grinned as she glanced away, sure her blush was darkening. If he'd said that to her a year or so ago, it'd have floored her. She looked back at Shaun as he turned to Lexi and Dylan.

"Ok, you two love birds, all is set for Saturday. I know its grand final day, but are you available?"

Lexi swallowed a mouthful of tea and nodded, a luminous smile on her face.

Dylan dipped his head. "We'll be there. Are you ready?"

Shaun sucked in a deep breath and blew it out. "I reckon I am." He looked on edge, but in a good way.

Hope looked between the three of them. What were they talking about? "Ready for what?"

Shaun looked like it was Christmas morning and Hope couldn't help but smile back at him. She glanced at Lexi, who was grinning ear to ear. Shaun tucked his wallet into the back pockets of his jeans then tossed his keys from hand to hand.

"I'm going to ask Renee to marry me. Saturday, after church, I've booked a table at our favorite restaurant, with the families nearby so we can celebrate together afterwards."

Hope felt the wind knocked from her lungs.

"What if she says no?" Dylan teased, wrapping an arm around Lexi's waist.

Shaun shot Dylan a less than amused look. "No chance."

"Confident. Is she expecting it?"

"Nope." Shaun shook his head. "She's been flat out with her studies. But since her exams have finished, I thought I'd play the surprise card."

Hope blinked when Shaun looked back at her, trying to find something to say. Her mouth dropped open, but congratulations just wouldn't come. After a moment, Shaun said his goodbyes to Lexi and Dylan. With one last glance at Hope and a quick good-bye, he left the room. Once the front door shut, Hope turned to Lexi and Dylan.

"Wow. Did not see that coming." She laughed through the crushing sensation within her chest. Shaun getting married? Why did it shock her? After all, he had been with Renee for years.

God, please tell me I don't still have feelings for him. Why couldn't I congratulate him?

Lexi smiled a cringe-like grin. "You ok?"

Hope swept a hand over the bench, distracted. "Yeah. Yeah, I'm great." Hope knew her voice was too high-pitched to be believable, so she flashed her trademark smile and deflected. "So, last night. Catch me up, guys. What did I miss?"

FORTY-TWO

"Welcome to Adventist Volunteers, you're speaking with Rose. How may I help you?"

Hope took a seat inside the sunlit reception area while a pleasant-looking woman spoke to someone making enquires over the phone. Probably someone like her.

The feeling of being on the edge of a precipice swept over her, and she read the motivational prints and framed Bible verses hanging on the walls. Never would she have seen herself heading down this road in life. She'd been sure her destiny was a career in fashion, not volunteering in an aid agency.

A collage of pictures caught her eye. While the soft-spoken conversation continued in the background, Hope rose to look at the photographs. Face after face of different nationalities smiled back at her from an array of settings—beaches, indoors, mountainous, building sites, concerts, backyards. She could tell there was an incredible story behind every photo. Heart fluttering,

Hope laid a hand over her chest as she examined the pictures. She wanted to be in those photos. To share in those stories, to help spread those smiles.

"Good morning."

Hope tore her eyes from the photographs and looked over to the front desk. The pleasant lady was looking expectedly back at her, her hands clasped over the desk with a warm smile lighting her expression. Hope turned to face her. "Hi. I'm Hope Meyer."

"Ah, Hope. Yes, I remember speaking with you on the phone. Have you had a chance to go through our webpage yet?"

A thrill ran through Hope. She still couldn't believe such incredible opportunities lay right under her nose, opportunities she'd never heard about before, opportunities that certainly didn't come up in her job search app.

Mind a buzz with what her future might look like if she was successful down this path, she might actually have found her career. A vibrant, exciting, useful career. "Yes, Rose, I have. I couldn't believe the opportunities. I mean, not that I'm not qualified for all of them, but more people should know about this."

"The Lord unveils His plans at the right time." Rose stood and came around the front of the reception desk, the aura coming from her was warm, comfortable, and inviting, like sitting around the dining table for a Sunday roast. "Many times, we've found that the right people have come to us at just the right time. It's incredible to watch the Lord at work. So, tell me, what were you interested in?"

"I love the look of the media and hospitality missions. I don't have formal skills, but I'm very good with tech and love helping people—apparently my gifts are giving and serving."

Rose chuckled as she straightened up an advertising poster on the front desk, before making her way back to her computer. "I was about to ask if you had done a spiritual gifts test."

Hope moved towards the reception counter, feeling at home in the lady's presence. "My minister suggested I complete the SHAPE course. That was interesting."

Rose began typing on the computer. "Oh, that is great. Excellent. Can you send me the details of your results? There are two short-term assignments within Australia for tech support at a rural church as they set up for an evangelistic campaign, and one for a hospitality worker for a busy lifestyle retreat. I already have your resume on hand, so I'll pop in applications for both. Then we'll get you started on the paperwork, so if you're successful in one of these positions you'll already have some runs on the board."

Hope's heart thumped. She nodded, watching the furious speed at which Rose's fingers moved over the keyboard.

No longer was she on the edge. She was plunging headfirst into the unknown.

* * * *

A sense of lightness filled Hope's spirit as she drove away from the Adventist Volunteers office. She had to talk to her friends, and it couldn't wait until youth night. She pulled her car over and sent out a quick group message.

'Guys, I have great news! Who's free?'

While waiting for replies, Hope signed into her job search app and removed her profile. There was nothing they could offer her. With a squeal and wiggle in her car seat, Hope opened up her social media to post about an exciting life change was about to happen, when the first of replies came through and she opened her messages instead.

Twenty minutes later, Hope pulled up at the main Beach. After locking up her car, she hurried towards the steps leading down towards the sand shimmering in the late afternoon sun. Lexi had the picnic rug set up and was unpacking a basket as she approached. Unable to hold in her excitement, she jogged the rest of the way.

Lexi looked up as she approached, smiled, and stood. "What's this great news? Are you and Josh back on?"

Hope laughed as she came to a stop before Lexi and hugged her. "No, no. That would be fantastic news. Where are the boys?"

"Dylan said this called for a pack of greasies, so you know where he is."

Hope plopped herself down on the picnic rug and laughed. "Yes, I can imagine."

"Nick and Trent are on their way." Lexi took a seat on the rug. "Do I have to wait until they get here, or can you give me the details now?"

Unable to hold it in any longer, Hope spilled everything she'd been wanting to talk to Lexi about. From doing the SHAPE program, to finding out her gifts, how the homeless shelter night impacted her, how conversations with Dave had led her to the meeting she'd just had.

"So you're going to be a ... missionary?"

Hope laid a hand over her forehead and stared back at Lexi. Hearing someone say it back to her drove the gravity of the situation home all the more. She nodded, dumbstruck. "Yep. I guess so."

A moment later, Lexi launched herself at Hope in a bear hug. Hope hugged her best friend back, and a surge of happiness swelled within her. Tears of pure happiness overflowed, and she sniffed as she let out a choked laugh. Lexi sat back and Hope rubbed her nose, seeing happy tears shining back at her in Lexi's eyes.

"This is so huge, Hope. I can't begin to express how proud I am of you, or how awesome God is to have brought you to this place."

Hope nodded. Words, for once, would not come. Overwhelmed at the new direction her life was taking, she could do nothing but smile.

FORTY-THREE

The evening was mild without a breath of wind, and the stars twinkled breathtakingly against the licorice sky. It was a perfect night for youth night at the beachside carnival.

Hope and Lexi were stationed at the entrance to the park, checking off the teens as they passed. Once all were accounted for, Hope and Lexi joined the boys gathered just inside the gates.

"Are you ready for a fun night?" Lexi shoulder bumped Hope.

"There's a rhetorical question if I've ever heard one," Dylan said dryly.

Hope grinned as she turned her gaze to the carnival and rubbed her hands together. "Am I ever." There were rides, food vans, sideshows, live band, the multicolored string lights that draped over the length of the main thoroughfare. She loved the annual spring carnival; it was always full of fun and unexpected moments. She turned back to her friends. "What are we waiting for? Let's get into it!"

Dave chuckled and held up his hands, "Just hold up a moment, Hope. It's the same deal as with every monthly social. Keep an eye on the youth, and remember your witness. Have fun, guys."

Dylan draped an arm over Lexi's shoulders, just as Dave ambled off to a group of youths calling out to him. "Well, we're off for a walk."

Lexi grinned and slipped an arm around Dylan's waist. Hope rolled her eyes, "Yeah right. To the Ferris wheel, I bet."

"The Ferris Wheel?" Lexi's voice was hushed as she glanced up at Dylan, who returned her comment with a mischievous grin and a wink. He looked back up at Hope, Nick and Trent. "We'll catch up with you all later."

Open-mouthed, Hope watched Dylan and Lexi disappear into the crowds before turning to Nick and Trent. "Boys?"

"Hey Nick!" A female voice called out, and Hope turned to the direction it came from when Nick moved between her and Trent.

"Excuse me, kids."

Hope had never seen Nick move so quick. She leaned into Trent while she watched Nick disappear into the crowds. "Well, I guess we won't be seeing much of Nick now Alice is here."

Moments later, Nick returned with his arm around Alice and a grin that spoke louder than words. Hope took in their knowing smiles as Trent chuckled. "Nice to see you again, Alice."

Hope pulled her phone out. "Oh hey, Alice, I gotta show you som—"

"No. No, you don't. She's got nothing to show." Nick began to steer his girlfriend away from Hope, while she made a weak attempt to wiggle out of his hold. "Aw, c'mon. I wanna see." Alice craned her neck towards what Hope was trying to show her.

"We're off. Sorry, Hope. You know, three's a crowd and all..." Nick gave a mock apologetic shrug. Hope glared at him as he turned Alice away, and they soon disappeared into the milling people. Hope huffed, pocketed her phone, and looked at Trent.

They were alone now. The thought shot through her mind to ask him the questions that had been burning in her mind. Would he talk, now it was just the two of them? What if she was way off base? A burst of adrenaline shot through her as she considered her options.

Hope lowered her eyes to the dusty path beneath her sandaled feet. "So … um …"

"G'day, Hope."

Hope whirled around to see Scott ambling towards her. "Hey! You came."

An unutterable thankfulness flooded her body for the interruption, and Hope turned to Trent while holding a hand out to Scott. "Trent, this is Scott, from work."

Trent closed the distance between them, holding out his hand. "Welcome."

Watching while the two men spoke, a surge of happiness overrode the suspicious thoughts about Trent that had been clouding her mind recently. Scott had known for years that she went to church and was a leader with the youth program, but he'd never wanted to know more than the basics. But he was here. He had responded to her invitation.

Although it was odd that Liam seemed more interested, even though he was new. Maybe she should have invited him too? Hope's smile dimmed at the thought of Liam, and she turned her gaze towards the carnival around her. What was he doing? He and his sisters had probably missed out on things like this – that thought sat heavily within her, while his comments about what she would do differently if she knew differently, came back to her mind.

"Sorry, fellas. I have to duck off for a second. Trent, can you babysit Scott for me?"

Scott chuckled and Trent gave a short nod.

"Great! I'll be right back." Hope turned and pulled out her phone while she walked. She found a quiet place behind the sideshows, opened her contacts, and found Liam's number under work colleagues. Taking a deep breath, she pressed the call button. He picked up after the third ring.

"There's a name I didn't think I'd see on my phone screen again."

Hope grinned as she looked over the lit car park. "How are you?"

"Good. Good. Sorry to hear you've moved on to bigger and better things."

Hope felt an eyebrow twitch. What story had Rob circulated about her leaving? What story had Claudia circulated? "Yeah, it was time to move on. But, that's not why I called. What are you and your family doing tomorrow evening?"

The sound of Liam clearing his throat came down the line. "Ah, Saturday nights are pretty quiet—I'm sure you know why. My sisters are still in high school, so I'm guessing they'll just be hanging altogether in the van."

"And you?"

"Just hanging out in my van. Why?"

Hope bit her lip through the smile on her face. "Well. I'm buying you and your family tickets to the Carnival for tomorrow night."

Silence came down the line and Hope felt her smile waver. "Liam?"

"You don't need to do that, Hope."

"Yes, I do. I want to. The tickets will be waiting for you all at the front gate entrance. The fireworks display scheduled for tomorrow night is something special. You guys will love it."

The line went silent once again, though this time Hope waited it out. The carnival was in full swing, and she spotted Scott and Trent talking with Dylan and Lexi. Scott had an easy smile on his face and looked comfortable with her friends. She loved seeing people she'd invited to youth or to church enjoying themselves. Contented, she turned away. Even though she figured Liam was still processing the unexpected gift, she spoke into his silence. "Liam, I just wanted to say thank you. You've impacted me in more ways than you could ever imagine."

She heard his soft exhale and imagined him smiling.

"Thanks, Hope, and right back at you. Just remember, there are people out there who will judge you when they find out your past. Don't listen to them. You're not that person anymore."

Hope smiled. After saying their goodbyes, she hung up and stared at her phone for a moment. Was he talking about her, or himself?

"Hope!" She turned back to the carnival to see Lexi waving her over. There was a youth night waiting, and a visitor was among them. Gently, she pushed the thoughts of Liam and his family aside—and the fact she'd probably never see him again—and headed towards the front gate to organize tickets for his family.

"Hey, Hope, over here!" Lexi called out.

Hope turned and walked backwards. "I'll be right there. Just gotta sort something out first."

FORTY-FOUR

Hope strode down Main Street, loving the sound of her heels on the footpath and the swish of her peach tea-length dress as she passed the bustling nightlife. Not a breath of wind blew, and the air had a hint of warmth about it said summer was on its way. It was a perfect night to be out celebrating the Tigers back-to-back premiership wins, and she was feeling good about Josh asking her to join him tonight.

Life looked and felt different already, and she was loving it. Home felt better too, with less noise and less things vying for her attention. Her mind felt clearer, and while her make-up drawer was severely diminished, she had more money for other things—like saving to buy another car.

The Beachside was at capacity with people standing shoulder to shoulder at the bar, and the dining room was bustling. As Hope made her way through to the alfresco area where Josh said he'd be waiting, Bec burst out from between a group of people.

"Hello, you!" Bec threw her arms around Hope and rocked her around in a circle. "I wasn't sure if you'd come tonight after last weekend's game. There seemed to be something bothering you." A look of empathy crossed Bec's features, and Hope found herself wanting to open up to the girl.

Josh appeared, drinks in hand and greeted her with a kiss on the cheek. "Hi."

Surprised at the catch in her breath, Hope managed a breathy hello back as Bec looked between the two of them. Josh's smile said more than words ever could. Hopefully Bec would take the hint.

Josh leaned towards her, his eyes were alight with a cheekiness that thrilled her. "I'll go give the fellas their drinks, then grab you one. I'll be right back."

"Thanks, I'll have a—"

"A drink for Hope, Bec." Josh said over his shoulder as he wove his way back into the crowd of people."

Hope bit her lip through a laugh as Bec tilted her head at her. "I heard you two had broken up?"

A giddy sensation began to weave its way into Hope's limbs. She nodded, trying to think how to explain what had recently been happening between her and Josh.

"Why did you break up? Did he hear about the homeless shelter thing?" Bec burst into loud laughter, steadying herself against Hope's shoulder. What was so funny about the homeless shelter? Had Bec always been this abrasive?

Hope tried to hide her disgust at Bec's mockery, disengaging the girl's hand before turning towards the bar to find Josh. If only they had caught up somewhere else.

A heavy arm fell across her shoulders. "That is some dress, Ms. Meyer."

Hope rolled her eyes as she elbowed herself out of Max's boozy side embrace.

Max slipped around in front of her. "Hey, I hear you're a single woman now." His tone was suggestive as his hands found her hips.

"Don't believe everything you hear." Hope moved out of his hold andstepped around him, conscious of what Josh would think if he saw Max hanging off her again. She could feel him right behind her as she maneuvered her way through the throngs of people.

"My source is very reliable."

"Are they?" Hope stopped, unable to move further. She could see they were close to the bar. Max's head appeared in her peripheral vision and she felt his cheek against hers. She jerked her head away and scowled at him, but he was looking forward. A cocky grin lit his features as he straightened, and his arm curled around her waist. "I still can't believe you let this one go, man."

Josh's gaze moved from Max to her, unreadable. He held out the drink he'd brought back for her. Hope pushed Max's arm off her hip and reached out to take the drink.

"She let me go." Josh's gaze moved back to Max, a pained expression on his face as he moved away into the crowd.

Dread curled in Hope's gut as she elbowed Max out of the way and took off after Josh. His large frame made a slip stream to follow, making it easier for her to pass through the crowd.

When they reached the less-occupied alfresco area, Hope drew in a long deep breath and took a seat beside Josh. He seemed tense now. Ignoring the flutter of butterflies within her stomach, she put her glass on the table.

"Why do I get the feeling you're annoyed about something?"

Josh sat back in his seat and rubbed his forehead. "I know what you told me that afternoon at your home, but seeing you and Max mucking around together again … I just … I dunno."

Hope sat forward on her seat. "I wasn't mucking around with him. I was looking for you, and he followed me."

A moment passed before Josh dropped his hand and he lifted his eyes to her. "He looked pretty snug behind you."

Hope thumbed toward the bar. "Didn't you see how many people were crowding the bar? I could barely get through."

Josh reached for his drink. His silence gnawed within her. They'd been over this ground before, but she now knew he was reacting from a place of hurt. Hope willed herself to calm the fight mode that rose up within. "Look, there's nothing I can do if you're set on holding the past against me. End of the day, I'm here to see you. Not Bec, not Max, not anyone else. I want to be with you."

There was so much more Hope wanted to say, but the atmosphere didn't allow. Josh downed his drink and replaced the glass on the table. He rubbed his jaw. "Hope, I don't know if I can go down that path again."

Heat formed behind her eyes and Hope looked down at her hands.

God, how could this happen? I thought everything was leading towards us getting back together.

A flood of noise spilled into the alfresco area. A group of players and partners stepped out from the bar and into the evening air, their expressions full of energy. With a sigh, Hope looked back at Josh. She didn't want to stay here any longer. "Ok. Well, I'm going to go."

Before Josh could say anything, Hope was out of her seat and heading towards the exit. Her thoughts warred beneath her smile. Things she wanted to say played over in her mind, while a quiet understanding tried to cool the fire in her stomach.

Her anger began to dissipate as she pushed through the main doors into the cool of the evening beyond the Beachside. Hope looked up and down Main Street, unsure what her next move would be. She'd been anticipating this evening all week, anticipating ending it wrapped in Josh's arms once again, but now she felt lost and confused.

Help me, God. Right now! What do I do?

The nearby crash of the ocean sounded in her ears against the hum of noise along Main Street. Taking a few steps along the footpath, she looked down a narrow-picketed walkway that led out onto the sand and the water beyond. The water seemed to always call to her. The beach was one place she felt both the peace and power of God. Decided, Hope turned down the sandy path towards the beach.

To spend time with God.

FORTY-FIVE

Bathed in the full moon, Hope made her way to the waters' edge and hugged her arms to herself as she looked up and down the empty foreshore. The sand looked to be aglow under the light of the full moon, and the blackened water twinkled. All was peaceful, with the distant hum of parties and music along Main Street filling the air with their merriment. With a sad shake of her head, she lowered her eyes to where the water rolled up along the sand. Once again, the night had played out differently than what she had imagined. Was she so disillusioned?

Frustrated, Hope kicked her heels off. Lifting the hem of her dress, she took a few steps towards the ocean. The icy water lapped against her toes, and she gave a soft yelp of shock. But it cleared her thoughts, and she stepped further in, her eyes heavenward.

"Oh, God I'm a mess. Whatever do you see in me? What do you want me to do? Am I even on the right track?"

"Hope?"

Hope gasped and whirled around. Water splashed further up her legs, and she yelped again. The male voice was familiar, but the shape of the silhouette didn't tell her who it was. The man continued towards her, and she soon recognized his soft chuckle. Her heart began thumping. "Shaun?"

He drew closer until the moonlight illuminated his features. Standing just back from the water's edge, he ran a hand over his head, his hair slipping through his fingers like thick silken treacle. She blinked.

"Yeah. It's me. You sound as shocked to see me here as I was to see you. Were you talking to yourself just a moment ago?"

Hope drew in a calming breath and blew it out. "Yeah, I … I was praying, actually." She laughed. "Why are you here? Isn't this your big night? Where's Renee?"

Shaun stood motionless for a moment, his focus turned beyond her as if he was lost in thought. "I don't know," he said with a deep sigh.

Another lap of water splashed up the back of her legs. Hope gasped at the cold and she trotted out of the water. "What happened?"

A contemptuous sniff came from Shaun as he looked away down the moon bathed foreshore. "I don't know."

The roar of the ocean filled the silence between them, mirroring the wild thoughts within Hope's mind. She wanted to go to him, but a warning within her conscience warned her to hang back. She figured he was looking towards the Mariners. The balcony lights were on, and she could see people enjoying a drink in the open air. Were they part of his party? Unable to quell her curiosity any longer, Hope stepped closer to him and placed a hand on his arm. "What happened?"

Shaun looked at where her hand lay on his arm, before lifting his eyes to hers. Her stomach quivered. He was so handsome. His casual suit and dark broody mood added to the energy emanating from him. A moment passed before he turned to face her, and she realized they had never spoken in such close quarters before.

"Renee said no."

The gravity of what he said broke through the daze his hazel eyes had grasped her in, and she blinked. "No? How is that possible?"

"I asked the question. She looked at me, grabbed her bag, and left."

"Maybe she needed a moment?"

"I waited over half an hour for her to come back."

"Maybe she needed longer than a moment."

"I've called a dozen times." Shaun thrust his hands into his pockets. "No answer and no returned calls."

"That still doesn't mean no. Maybe she's overwhelmed. You did say she's only just finished her exams ..."

Shaun let out a soft exhale as he looked out over the water again. "I appreciate what you're trying to do. But I think the ship's sailed. I didn't know what to do, so I thought I'd wander the foreshore." Shaun turned back towards the ocean before slumping down into the sand. "This isn't how I imagined the night would go."

Hope looked at his dejected form and her heart went out to him. Not to the same degree, but she knew how he felt. His heart was broken too. Gathering up her dress, Hope lowered herself onto the sand next to him. "Yeah. I thought my night would turn out different too."

"Is that what you were down here praying about?"

"Yeah."

"Any answers?"

Hope lifted a handful of sand and watched the glittering crystals fall through her fingers. She wasn't sure. Her oldest crush was less than an arm's length from her, they were alone at night on a moonlit beach, and the conversation was moving to a level beyond their normal flirty banter—and he was a Christian. Did

God close the door with Josh because He had something better planned for her? Like Shaun? Her chest tightened at the thought. "I'm not sure. But tomorrow's a new day, as Trent likes to tell me."

"You know," Shaun angled his torso towards her and rested an arm over his knee. "It's interesting that I ran into you here though."

A soft breeze blew in off the water and Hope tucked a strand of hair behind her ear. "Why is that?"

Shaun offered a lopsided grin. "You've always had a way of cheering me up."

She had no idea she'd had that effect on him. "Thanks. I guess."

"When I left the Mariners, I couldn't see beyond the next minute. But I ran into you, and …"

Shaun let the sentence hang as his eyes travelled her face. When they lingered at her mouth, she turned away. She sensed where this was headed. How many times had she prayed for this very moment with this man? So why did it have to come now? The guy was broken, and if she hung around any longer, she'd be more than willing to put him back together. She had to lighten the mood, somehow.

"Maybe it's a gift." She tried to inject a cheeky tone into her words as she glanced back at him.

His stare held. "Maybe it's just you."

A heaviness pooled in her limbs at the intensity shinning behind his eyes combined with the rugged note in his voice. All of a sudden, a jovial ringtone pierced the charged space between them. With a shaky hand, Hope felt for her bag and shoes, and fished her phone out of her bag, grateful for the interruption.

The phone stopped ringing, but there was no notification of a missed call. She frowned, then put the phone back in her bag, and pushed herself up. "Shaun. I gotta go." Her voice broke as she tried to speak past the rolling sensation within her body. Taking a step backwards, Hope willed the strength to come back into her joints.

Raucous laughter broke out somewhere along Main Street. Hope glanced towards the Beachside before turning back to Shaun. He was on his feet and took a step towards her.

"Why? I could really use some company."

Taking another step back, Hope gave a slight shake of her head as if answering the pleading in her mind to go to him. "Because I think you need to go and find Renee."

Shaun pocketed his hands as he dropped his gaze. A moment passed before Hope saw his shoulders droop and he gave a slow nod. A lump formed in her throat and biting her lip, she turned away. Laying a hand over her mouth, Hope drew in a ragged breath as she made her way back to Main Street.

FORTY-SIX

ope reached the concrete footpath of Main Street and dusted the sand off her feet before slipping her heels back on. Straightening, she blinked against the tears forming and wiped the tip of her nose. She just wanted to be home.

It would have been wrong if she'd stayed on the beach with Shaun, and she needed to remind herself of that. There'd be a reason why Renee ran out on Shaun. Hope began the walk home at pace, not slowing as she wove around people meandering along the footpath, ignoring the jovial conversations and laughter spilling out from the alfresco restaurants.

She should be having a night like that.

She and Josh should be back together.

A figure emerged from under a shop front before her on the footpath and she gasped, her hand flew to her chest. She froze. "What are you doing here?"

Trent pocketed his phone as he moved towards her. "You ok?"

Hope took a step back from Trent and shook her head as she looked back from where she'd come. She couldn't look at him. The thoughts in her head began to tumble out as the tears she was trying to hold slipped down her cheeks.

"I don't know. I'm crazy about Josh, so what is it that gets me when I'm around Shaun? I thought I was over him. I went to the beach to spend time with God. Then he shows up!" Her hand held a tremor as she gestured near her head. "And these thoughts in my mind wouldn't stop, and they didn't seem like me but were in my voice. To be with him, to help him feel better—and not just by talking …"

As Hope laid a hand over her mouth and closed her eyes as if to shut out the images in her mind, she felt Trent's hands grasp her upper arms.

"Hope. Listen to me."

Startled by the strength in his hold on her, Hope opened her eyes to find him stooped to her height; his vibrant green eyes boring into hers.

"The enemy knows us better than we know ourselves. He knows your past feelings about Shaun. He knew what was happening with you and Josh, and he knew what was happening with Shaun and Renee tonight. He engineered tonight so you'd meet at your lowest points, anticipating that you both would fall. He speaks thoughts into people's minds in their own voices, to confuse and unsettle. He is the master deceiver, and he does this best by getting people to question themselves. Like you are, right now."

Trent released his grip and straightened. "He sets traps before people, but God is faithful. He will not let you be tempted beyond what you can bear. But when you are tempted, God will also provide a way out so you can endure it."

Hope drew in a ragged breath and rubbed her arms as she thought over what he'd said. It certainly made sense, and she couldn't deny the comfort that had come over her at his words.

Her phone ringing earlier was odd but gave her room to flee. She tilted her head, remembering Trent pocketing his phone. She narrowed her eyes at him.

"Why are you here? Visiting someone in the area?"

Trent gave a slow nod, though Hope didn't miss the twinkle in his eyes. Throwing caution to the wind, Hope took a step towards him, not dropping her gaze from his. They would have this conversation now. "Tell me something. Will Shaun and Renee make it?"

"Yes. But if you hadn't held up tonight, things would have been very different in the light of tomorrow."

Hope shivered at the reminder of how close she'd come to crossing that line, and losing her nerve, she dropped her gaze. "Maybe so, but not inside my head. That was intense. I don't even have to close my eyes and I see things, feel things …"

"Philippians 4:8. If a thought comes to mind that does not align with this, you need to pray it away."

A light breeze blew through the lace panels along the bottom of Hope's dress, and she watched the delicate material rippling in the breeze.

Pray the seductive thoughts away. Sounds so simple.

"Easier said than done, Trent." Hope looked back up at him.

His attention was focused in the opposite direction from where they'd come. Hope craned her neck to see if she could see what he was looking at, but Main Street looked the same as it had all night. She was about to ask what he was looking at when he turned to her, his manner uncharacteristically hurried, his expression focused.

"It gets easier. Just remember to ask Jesus for help. Listen, I gotta run. See you Monday night."

"Wait." Hope reached out a hand to him as he began to move off. "Where are you going?"

"Stay in prayer and head home."

As Trent jogged off, Hope turned toward home. Astronger breeze had began to blow and she held her dress down as she walked. Where could Trent be running off to? His phone hadn't rung, and nobody had called out to him.

The long walk home under a blanket of a million stars with the distant crash of the surf in her ears calmed Hope's spirit. She thought over what Trent had said while she walked. There were still some areas in her life she needed to do battle with.

The day she'd cancelled Netflix and overhauled her wardrobe had been so exhausting that she couldn't mentally bring herself to go through her books. Now at home, standing in front of her bookcases, the task seemed just as daunting. She loved her books. But some of these were filling her mind with the wrong ideas, giving subliminal suggestions, warping her perception, and weakening her defenses.

A muffled ringtone reverberated from her bag, but Hope ignored it. Too often, she allowed her phone to distract her from the job at hand.

Although it was ten-thirty on a Saturday night, too late to dig into culling her bookcase. Hope reached over to her desk and grabbed a hot pink sticky notepad and a pen.

Her phone rang again

Hope glanced at it, pen poised over the notepad. Odd. Who'd ring her back-to-back at this hour of the night? Quickly, she wrote Philippians 4:8 on the notepad and stuck the sticky note on the side of the bookshelf, then went to retrieve her phone. It dinged to say a message had been received.

Surprised to see two missed calls and a message from Lexi, she opened the phone to find out what was going on.

Jack's back in Winchester Parade Hospital after being attacked at home. We need to pray. Can you come ?'

Hope gasped. Her hand held a slight shake as she hit reply. *'I'm on my way.'*

FORTY-SEVEN

reathless, Hope came to an abrupt stop against the reception desk. Her nails dug into the wooden surface as she caught her breath. The receptionist opened the sliding window, a dubious look upon her face. "Can I help you, miss?"

"Jack. Saunders. Please."

The light sounds of keyboard tapping filled the quiet reception area. Hope straightened and looked around, anxious to get going.

"Room 32, level C."

"Thank you." Hope ran to the elevator. When the doors didn't open quick enough, she headed for the stairs. Taking the steps two at a time, she reached level C and burst through the hard door into a sterile corridor and tried to orientate herself. Medical staff rushed all around her, monitors beeped, and telephones rang. A nurse stopped to ask if she needed some help, and after a short chat Hope was off towards Jack's room.

As Hope approached, she noticed the door of the private room was ajar, and could hear soft intermittent conversation as it floated out into the hallway. Hope peered inside the room to see Jenny and Dylan close to the bed, while Lachlan and Lexi, Nick and Trent stood by. Lexi looked up and relief flashed over her face. Hope hurried to her side.

"What on earth happened?" Hope kept her voice hushed and angled herself towards Lexi.

Lexi hugged her arms. "Dylan thinks it was a professional hit. They don't know who, but Triple-zero responded to a call out for multiple stab wounds. There was no one home when they arrived, and Jack was unconscious, so they broke in. The hospital called Jenny and Dylan. Trent got here first. Nick has only just arrived."

"If it was a professional hit, wouldn't Jack be dead?" Hope felt a chill run up her spine.

"He's not far from it. I thought now we're all here, we could pray around his bed."

"Of course." Hope put an arm around Lexi and they moved with her towards the bed. Dylan's head came up as she approached. He offered a weak smile while Jenny blew her nose softly beside him. Hope's heart broke for Dylan and his family. If Jack knew this was where his decisions would lead him, would he have taken the first steps down this path?

A light knock on the door interrupted her thoughts and Dave entered. Dylan rose. "Everyone, thanks for coming."

Dave put a hand on Dylan's shoulder. "I've spoken to the nurses at the nurses' station. The prognosis is good—"

"But what happens when he gets home?" Jenny wailed. "They'll come back!"

Hope glanced around the room. Nick's expression was like steel as he and Dylan shared a look.

"Surveillance will be upped at your home, Mrs. Saunders." Nick spoke into the grim silence. "I know the team are getting close to an arrest. That is about all I can share with you at this time. However, if you'd feel more comfortable staying somewhere else, I could see what we could arrange. Off the record, I suspect this hit was done by a rookie. Your home will hold more clues, one of which may be the key to ending this."

Hope swallowed at the implication of Nick's words. She'd seen enough movies to understand what would happen to the rookie if word got back to their employer that Jack was still alive … and what would happen now.

"We were due in court later this week." Dylan was making a study of his clasped hands; his voice so hushed his mouth hardly looked to be moving. "He was going to give a statement about all he's seen, who he dealt with, who he delivered to. Plead guilty and be sentenced."

"Someone's nervous." Lachlan expressed everyone's thoughts.

Dylan sniffed and lifted his head to look at the man. "That's what I think."

Lexi laid a hand on Dylan's leg. "Could that mean you're a target? Like if someone thinks Jack told you stuff? Or one of us?"

Nick cleared his throat but remained silent. Hope toyed with her fingers as her mind played out a number of scenarios. "What should we do?"

Dave held a hand up. "Let's remember who is in charge here—God. So let's gather around Jack and, as the Bible says, come boldly before the throne, Let's lift Jack and his family up for protection, pray for the police to find the people responsible, and for peace to be over the Saunders home."

Joining hands with Lexi and Lachlan, Hope bowed her head and listened as Dave prayed over the situation. After Dave finished, one by one, they each offered a prayer for Jack and the situation. Goosebumps sprinkled Hope's arms as the prayers continued to flow from each bowed head. She heard movement in the room but kept her thoughts heavenward. It must be nursing staff monitoring vital signs. It would be far too easy to freak out right about now.

A long moment of silence followed the last prayer. Hope opened an eye and looked over each bowed head. Slowly she saw others opening their eyes, raising their heads and disengaging hands. In the exchanging of encouraging smiles with one another, Hope frowned. Where was Trent?

He was gone.

FORTY-EIGHT

Hope rolled onto her side and squinted against the sun streaming in her bedroom window. What time was it?

Her arm felt like concrete as she moved it from under the doona to reach for her phone, and her mouth felt like the bottom of a birdcage. Last night had been intense. She moistened her lips and brought the phone to her face.

11:13 a.m.

Hope's eyes widened. She hadn't slept in that late for a long time.

An envelope flashed in the corner of the phone screen, and she opened up her messages.

Lexi.

Hope felt her stomach tense. Was Jack ok? They'd stayed at the hospital long into the morning hours, praying over Jack and trying to comfort Jenny. Hope rubbed her eyes and opened the message. Her eyes widened all the more.

'Renee said Yes! My big bro is getting married. Join us for afternoon tea to celebrate. 2:30. Love Lexi xx'

* * * *

Hope pulled up outside the Slaydon residence and pulled the handbrake on with more force than necessary. Cars were parked everywhere along the street and up Lexi's driveway. She wasn't sure what to expect. The din of celebrations coming from within her best friend's house floated around her, almost chafing within her consciousness. She was thrilled, but her gut was churning.

What would she say to Shaun?

A million questions circled in her mind, but she couldn't grasp one of them to follow the line of thought. She was tired and felt like a space cadet from lack of sleep. Resigned to whatever the afternoon brought, Hope got out of her car, locked it, and headed inside.

"Love of my Life" by Harry Styles spilled over the threshold as Hope opened the front door and her hand tightened on the door handle. Heart-shaped helium balloons hung from the ceiling and "I do" printed confetti littered the carpet. Did she bring up what almost happened last night, or let it go? What would she say to Shaun when they would no doubt run into each other?

The door closed with a click behind her, and Hope made her way down the hallway, through balloon ribbons, toward the open living area and the sounds of the party.

"Oh, you're here!" Lexi threw her arms around Hope drawing a smile from her. Returning the embrace Hope thanked God Lexi found her before she found Shaun. "Of course I'm here. How did you pull together a celebration so quickly? What time did you guys get back from the hospital?"

Lexi stepped back from Hope. "Oh, I think it was after five." Lexi waved a hand over the room. "Renee did all this. She turned up a little after nine and started decorating the place."

Hope felt her mouth drop open. "Renee?"

Lexi signaled Hope to follow her as she headed back down the hallway to the loungeroom at the front of the house. Hope followed, muffling a yawn. Was she awake, or was this some strange dream she'd wake from any minute?

The loungeroom was bathed in the afternoon sun. The feeling in the room as vibrant as the smile on Lexi's face as she moved aside some balloon streamers. "So last night, Shaun asked Renee to marry him, and she just up and left. We all came out from where we were waiting to find out what happened. Shaun said he had no idea. We waited for a good half an hour before Shaun got up and left. I've never seen him so sad. When he didn't come back, we disbanded and went home. No one knows where he went, but apparently when he went home, she was there. The place was full of candles, and their favorite songs were playing. Soon as he walked in, she proposed to him!"

This was definitely a dream. Hope scratched the back of her head. "Wow. That's ... a story."

Happy laughter bubbled out of Lexi as she clapped her hands. "I know. It's so Shaun and Renee."

"But when did she call all these people?"

"Last night. After she left the Mariners. She teed it all up for this afternoon as a surprise. C'mon. Let's get back to the party. She even managed to find a caterer at the last minute."

Still feeling like she was playing catch up, Hope followed Lexi back to the party just as "Fall into Me" by Forest Blakk floated down the hallway towards them. How was she supposed to join this party? The music grated and she felt awkward knowing what had almost happened with Shaun last night.

"Hope, you got a sec?"

Hope started at Shaun's voice beside her. Though her stomach bottomed out, she turned to him and tilted her head. "What's up?"

He lowered his voice as he leaned towards her. "I just wanted to thank you. I was ruined last night, and I'm not sure what would have happened if you didn't tell me to go and find Renee—"

Hope bit her tongue as Shaun was turned around by a party-goer, who gave Shaun a few hard raps on his shoulder and laughed loudly. An uncle or work colleague? Either way, she sensed the conversation wasn't going to be a quick one, and she wanted to try some of the delicious food she could smell in the room.

Hope wove her way through the living room and over to the kitchen where she found trays of canapes set out in heart shapes over the candle and confetti-decorated benchtops. The pecan cream and small pear brownies looked delicious, and Hope's mouth watered in anticipation.

Shaun stepped into her line of vision. "Hey, sorry about that…"

Withdrawing her hand, Hope turned her attention to Shaun. There would be another interruption any minute, and there were things that needed to be said.

"It's ok. I know you were in a bad place last night. I wasn't in a good place either. I'm just happy that … nothing happened …"

Shaun looked down, but she saw the impish grin play upon his mouth. "Yeah. Me too."

"Have you told Renee?"

He looked up with a nod of his head. "Yeah. We had a long talk about it. She's ok. She understands."

"Good to hear. It was a shock this morning to hear you two were engaged, but I'm thrilled for you both."

As people began to gather around and pick at the canapes, Hope selected a brownie and with a quick smile at Shaun, moved to make her way back into the room. With Lexi cozied up to Dylan, Nick and Trent unable to attend, the room was filled with love. Hope just wanted to go home and lick her wounds. Last night had been emotionally draining.

She was just about to pop the brownie in her mouth when Shaun caught up with her again. "I just want to say, before we get anymore interruptions, that you're an incredible woman, Hope. And thank you for … for saving me from myself."

The look on his face was one of vulnerability. She had never seen this side of him before, yet it struck her that she'd been the victim of the same temptation. Just as Trent had said. Her heart softened.

"That wasn't me. That was God. He saved us from ourselves."

FORTY-NINE

ope sat in the quiet of the family home and drummed her fingers over the living room coffee table. About this time on a normal Monday, she'd be out the back of House and Home, sharing weekend shenanigans with her work colleagues. Now she had nothing to do, and all day to do it in.

Restless, she clicked on the TV and absentmindedly surfed the channels before turning the TV off in frustration and moving to the kitchen to raid the fridge. No sooner had she opened the fridge door than she closed it and growled to herself. The gnawing sensation within her wasn't going to be satisfied by something sweet.

Unsure what to do with herself, Hope wandered from the kitchen, down the hall and into the lounge. Just over a week ago, she and Josh had shared such an intimate conversation here, one that left her sure they'd get back together. As her mind went over the events of Saturday night once again, the crushing sensation of him not wanting her crashed over her anew.

Just then, her phone began ringing from where it lay on the bench in the kitchen. Desperate for something to cling to in her sinking thoughts, Hope broke into a jog and reached the phone by the fourth ring. "Hello, Hope speaking." Her voice chirped despite her despair.

"Hope. Hello. It's Rose from Adventist Volunteers. How are you?"

Hope took a seat on the kitchen table and drew her legs up to rest on the seat next to her. "I'm great! How are you?"

A light chuckle came down the line. "I am well. Hope, I call with wonderful news. Remember I submitted your application to a rural church seeking tech support for their upcoming evangelism meetings? The pastor loves your resume and wants to schedule an interview."

"Oh." Hope jumped off the table. "Oh, that's great." Hope tried to keep her voice controlled but she couldn't believe it. Soft laughter came down the line and Hope giggled, "Sorry."

"That's ok dear. Now the interview is next Monday at nine. I will email you the Zoom link for you to meet with Brian and Karen from the church, online. They were very impressed with your resume and SHAPE results and are looking forward to speaking with you."

Hope tried to reign in her smile so she could phrase a sentence. "Thank you, Rose. I'll have my computer charged up and ready to go."

"Have a great week, Hope. Good luck for next Monday, we will be praying for you."

The line when dead and Hope stood, frozen to the spot, staring at her phone screen. Processing. A burst of excitement erupted within her and she screamed, hopped on the spot then took off at full speed down the hall and jumped onto the couch with another scream.

Breathless, Hope flopped onto the couch and ran a hand over her hair. The feeling of utter contentment settled into her bones as she caught her breath. Nothing had ever felt so right—and she hadn't even got the job yet. Just the interview; just the idea of going on a mission trip, just the concept of going away to help someone she didn't even know, rang so loud and clear deep within her, she could do nothing else but sit and smile. She knew her direction now.

Ok, God. Where to from here? What do I do now? Please talk to me.

A breeze blew through the loungeroom curtains, bringing with it the sweet salty scent of the ocean. Not a cloud in the sky blocked the brilliant late spring sunshine. She rose from the couch.

"Ivory, girl. Time for a run."

* * * *

The beach was almost empty as Hope unclipped Ivory's lead and watched the dog run off towards the waves. A flock of birds took off from the water as Ivory ran into the water, her happy barks echoing back up the foreshore. Hope sent a smile heavenward. One week from now, and she would be having a life-changing interview. What would she do with herself between now and then? She wished the interview was tomorrow.

A figure jogging down the beach drew her attention and she grinned. Trent. His jog was steady as he speared off from the waters' edge and jogged up the sand towards her.

"Morning, Hope."

"Hey there. Great morning for a jog."

Trent slowed his pace and walked the rest of the distance between them, his Mediterranean features were smooth like golden silk in the early morning sun. Even his dreadlocks had a glow. "I like to run in the morning, to spend time with God and let Him plan my day."

Hope had an overwhelming urge to ask where he disappeared to while they were gathered at Jack's bedside. But how would she phrase the burning question? Sometimes when he looked at her, she faltered. Her mind seemed to go blank. She ran her hands threw her hair, then ruffed up the back of her bob.

"Hey, I have an interview with Adventist Volunteers next Monday."

Trent stretched out a shoulder, and a broad smile further lit his features. "Great news, Hope. You heading off on a mission trip … Just another one of the many changes have been happening in you recently."

A laugh bubbled out of her, and she gave him a gentle shove. "Hold the phone. I haven't got the job yet … or do you know something I don't know?"

There was a twinkle in Trent's eyes before he looked away, stretching the other shoulder. Emboldened by his reaction, Hope took a step to face him and raised her eyebrows. "Well?"

Trent turned his intense gaze to her. "Let's just say, Jesus is doing a work within you. This is evident in the change we all see. You're wanting to embark on a life of giving of yourself, your time, your possessions. You're wanting to serve others in any way you can, people you don't even know. This is how Jesus shows Himself to those around you, through you using your gifts. They look at you, but see or feel Him. Your gifts of giving and service are two powerful gifts. And an interview is not where your story ends. It goes far beyond that."

Hope looked back at the water, considering what Trent had said. Last year, she'd no idea why she was called into the leadership program. She was just having fun. But in the light of what Trent said, she could see where Dave had her placed in the team and why youth was the highlight of her week. It was part of the good works she was created to do. Hope's eyes became gritty. She had been created with a purpose in mind!

Trent cleared his throat, and she looked back at him. "As the Psalmist said, 'delight yourself in the Lord and He will give you the desires of your heart.'"

Ivory barked and Hope looked for her dog. An elderly couple were throwing a stick for her. "It's funny. I used to think that text meant we can love God and still do whatever we want."

"Many people do think that. But no one knows you better than God. And when you decide to put Him first in life, He'll show you what will make you most happy and feel most satisfied."

Warmth radiated from her core at his words and spread through her limbs. He was right. She'd never have imagined her life heading in this direction, but now she couldn't picture anything else bringing as much happiness to her mind and heart. Not to mention, the things she once thought were fun … had her perspective changed that much? Had she changed that much?

"God is good." Trent murmured.

Hope looked heavenward again. "All the time."

"And all the time," Trent said, and Hope heard the smile in his voice.

"God is good." She looked at him.

He held up a hand and Hope high-fived him. "See you at leadership tonight?"

"I'll be there."

FIFTY

"Toothpaste?" Lexi's pen was poised over her run sheet. Hope rummaged through the shopping bag she'd brought to youth night. "Check."

"How's your week been? Spoons?"

"Boring!" Hope rearranged some items, searching for the bag of spoons. "Unemployment is not for me, I can tell you that. Ah, here they are. Check."

"Ready for your interview next week?"

Hope put the bag down she was pulling items out of and sighed. She'd spent the week rehearsing interview questions she'd found online and changed her interview outfit a number of times. "I think so."

Lexi cleared her throat. "If God has brought you down this path and opened the doors for you, then you can be confident this is where He is leading, so just be yourself."

Last-minute jitters had her in their grasp, and Satan was trying to buffet her; she knew it. The unrelenting nerves, the questions about if she really wanted to go down this line, did she really know that much about tech? Lexi's hand landed on hers. When Hope looked up, Lexi gave Hope a lingering smile of encouragement before looking back at her run sheet. "Do we have syringes?"

Hope hummed as she searched the bag. Seeing them, she pulled them out. "Check."

"Straws?"

"Check." Hope mentally kicked herself into gear. She knew tech like the back of her hand.

"Plates?"

"Check"

Mind back on the job, Hope smiled as she considered how the youth would receive this icebreaker. It had resonated with her.

"Ok, we're right for the icebreaker. Let's go set up." Lexi started scooping the items off the bench. Hope joined in, scooping up the remaining objects, and headed out into the hall. In no time, they had six tables set up. They placed a tube of toothpaste and a plate on each, along with some spoons, syringes, and straws. The boys entered just as they were finishing. Dylan headed to the kitchen with the night's supper items, while Nick and Trent crossed the room towards them.

"Dave's on his way." Nick looked around the room. "Anything else need doing?"

"Nope. All done." Lexi hefted herself up to sit on the edge of the stage.

The hall doors burst open. Hope's favorite part of the night had begun. Energy was high, expectation was radiating from every face, and laughter was merry. With a skip, she headed across the floor to welcome everyone as they joined in the fun.

Fifteen minutes later, Lexi had the room separated into six teams. Each team surrounded a table, quizzical expressions upon their faces as they looked at the items before them. Hope stood along the wall with the boys while Lexi explained the icebreaker. Hope loved watching everyone's faces, watching them morph from complete rapture at squeezing out the entire tube of toothpaste onto the plate, to complete bewilderment when Lexi explained they now had to get the toothpaste back into the tube using only the items on the table …and all before the timer sounded.

The mayhem that followed had Hope in stitches. Lexi said it would be messy, and she wasn't wrong. A cloying scent of peppermint filled the air. The toothpaste was going everywhere but back in the tube. It was over hands, over the tools, over the tabletops. Hope had been praying the teens would understand the message and not have to have a true-life experience like she had been having.

The timer sounded.

"Tools down." Lexi called. After a few moments of quieting down the residual excited chatter and giggles, Lexi continued. "James three verse ten says, 'out of the same mouth come praise and cursing. My brothers and sisters, this should not be.' Our words can lift people up, or cut them down. We can't do both. The things we say are powerful and can't be taken back … just like there's no way that toothpaste was going back into the tube. Think about how easy it was to squirt it out all over the plate. Words are easy to say, but impossible to take back. The effect remains even after we've apologized. Some of you may remember the banana surgery game we did earlier this year. When you leave here, remember who you represent in your communities and use your words wisely."

Hope dropped her head a moment, and asked God to forgive her before she joined in the cleanup. She knew He already had, but the guilt was still raw. How could she make right the wrongs she'd done? She'd misrepresented God and hurt people she loved.

A conversation wove its way into her prayerful state, and she raised her head in the direction of the voices she'd tuned into.

Melanie and Jade were giggling about antics at a local club last night and giving another girl, Sarah, tips on how to get a guy to ask her out.

"Do you think that'd work?" Sarah sounded unsure.

"Pretty sure. Let's ask Hope." Jade said, her voice held an enthusiastic note.

Hope's eyes widened just as the girls turned and headed for her. Before they could say anything, Hope motioned for them to follow her to the café.

Activities were gearing up in the hall behind them as Hope turned to face the girls. She caught the 'what are you doing?' face from Lexi, and gestured 'give me five minutes' before looking back at the girls faces before her. They stared at her like teacher's pets waiting to be praised for good work.

She needed to sit down for this, so she pulled out a chair and sat at one of the tables. The girls followed.

"Ok. I know you girls saw me at that club, dancing with a guy. I know you've watched me flit around the room, drawing attention to myself, making people laugh and generally being the center of attention and all that."

The girls nodded, but their puzzled faces showed they didn't get her point.

"Girls, I've been so wrong. I know you've looked up to me and I've encouraged you to. But, just like tonight's message showed, we can't take back the things we've said … or the things we've done."

This confession was harder than she'd thought.

"See, I'd be a terrible youth leader if I didn't share the hard lessons I've had to learn. Don't go down the path you're flirting with. It ends in disaster, lost friendships, and hurt."

A lump formed in Hope's throat, and she swallowed hard. The girls looked awkward, but she might save them from a fall if they got the message. Hope cleared her throat. "I'm sorry, girls. I don't want to dampen your night, but I had to apologize for being a horrible example, and I hope you don't try to copy me out there. Please."

"Girls. You joining us?"

Hope looked up. Nick passed a ball between his hands while Dylan waved them over. She nodded and waved the boys off before looking back at the girls. "Did that make sense?"

The girls nodded their heads slowly but without making eye contact. They looked uncomfortable. Had she messed up again? Would they stop coming to youth group now? Should she have kept quiet?

As soon as the thought came into her mind, swift peace followed. She'd done the right thing.

Hope rose from her seat. "Right then. Go join back in. I'm going to help Lexi get the café ready." Watching as the girls rose and made their way back to the group, Hope called after them. "Oh, Sarah…"

The girls turned, but Hope kept her eyes on Sarah. "The best way to get a guys attention, is to be confident."

Out of the corner of her eye, she saw Melanie and Jade elbow each other and share smug glances, while Sarah's gaze dropped to the floor.

"But the best way to keep a guy's attention …" Hope glanced at Melanie and Jade standing beside Sarah, just as Sarah raised her eyes to look back at her. A wave of compassion hit Hope as their eyes met.

God, please help my words to sink deep and take root and help Sarah not to fall.

Hope stepped towards her and placed a hand on Sarah's shoulder.

"Is to be real."

FIFTY-ONE

*H*ope pulled up in the church car park and shut off the engine. From her seat, she looked around to see if Melanie and Jade had arrived yet. Their conversation last night at youth had played over and over in her mind, breaking her sleep. Even her first wakeful thoughts were prayers they'd have taken the gentle rebuke in the manner it was meant—from sister to sister in Christ.

There was a tap on the window beside her just as she spotted Melanie and Jade among the group entering the church. Relieved, Hope let out a long breath and smiled, turning to see who tapped on her window.

"Hey." Josh straightened, took a step back from her door, and leaned back against his car.

Hope blinked. Frozen in her seat, she stared back at the man she'd been hoping and praying would come to church since their first meeting. She'd thought last Saturday night was the final nail in the coffin, so what was he doing at church? Dressed like he was actually coming to church? Was this a dream? Josh appeared to chuckle, then signaled for her to exit her car.

The hinge groaned under her palm as she pushed it open. Hope stepped out, her eyes never leaving Josh's. She closed the door and stepped back against it. "What are you doing here?"

"I thought the usual greeting was Happy Sabbath?"

Hope grinned as she glanced away. She'd often said that to him when she had caught up with him after church. With a nod of her head, she looked back at him. "Happy Sabbath, Josh. What are you doing here?"

Josh exhaled a long breath and shoved his hands into his pockets. She couldn't help but smile at his check shirt, dark navy jeans, and white casual shoes—an outfit unlike anything else she'd ever seen him wear. He was next-level handsome and for a fleeting moment, life felt like she'd prayed it to be for a long time.

He cleared his throat. "It was Kaitlyn's birthday party last night."

"So that's why she wasn't at youth. Was it a good night?"

Josh chuckled and nodded. "Yeah. She had a blast. Still can't believe my little sister is twenty-one."

Hope smiled through the heaviness in her heart at missing Kaitlyn's milestone birthday party. "Well, I'm really happy she had a great night. But that doesn't really answer my question about why you're here ..."

Josh acknowledged Hope's comment with a cheeky grin before his countenance turned focused. "One of Kaitlyn's new friends arrived wearing a unique coat. I've only seen one other person wear a coat like that in The Valley ..."

Hope lifted a shoulder and felt her brow crinkle. Did he come to church to discuss what someone she didn't know wore to a party she hadn't been invited to? "Ok. Not really sure what to do with that."

"We know the family. Their old man lost his business a few years ago and they live in the caravan park just out of town. There is no way they could afford a coat like that."

Hope felt her mouth drop open. Could it be … Had one of Liam's sisters found her coat in an op shop? A silence hung between them while Josh appeared to be considering adding to what he'd just said, when he nodded as if to encourage the line of thought she was on. Hope felt her mouth work as if to start forming words, but nothing came out. Josh came alongside her. His eyes held an earnest appeal, and she couldn't tear her gaze away.

"I knew it was your coat, Hope. And I know how much you paid for it."

Hope looked down, ashamed at how she used to spend her money. She examined the fine gravel of the car park, then Josh tipped her chin up to face him.

"Last Saturday night … I judged you. I saw you and Max, and instead of asking you about it, I made a call. The wrong call. I know you're a different person now and seeing this girl last night wearing the coat you must have given away just killed me. I had to come and see you and apologize."

Feeling her hand encased in his, Hope drew in a breath through parted lips. Words would not come. To donate that coat was one of the hardest things she'd done. But she'd felt so incredible afterwards, she'd thought that was the blessing.

This was unexpected.

Josh's fingers entwined around hers. "Can we try again?"

The words she had been longing to hear, finally murmured in that husky tone of his. They sent her pulse racing and her mouth felt dry. Her mind flashed back to last Saturday night when she thought the door had closed between them and her chance meeting with Shaun. She shook her head. Trent had said if she didn't hold up, things would have been very different— obviously he had meant not just for Shaun.

"Hope?" Josh's thumb ran over the back of her knuckles. "I'm sorry I hurt you. I wanna go back to last Saturday night and—"

"No." Surprised by how strong her voice came out despite the shaking she felt inside, Hope gripped Josh's hand. "No. I'm sorry I hurt you. I have missed you so much, I'm not sure I believe this moment is happening. But yes. Yes, of course I want to try again."

Laughter bubbled out, surprising her and drawing a laugh from him.

"Josh, I never wanted the break in the first place, but I'm thankful you called it. Even though it's been horrible, I've learned so much. I have a plan now, and it's brought me closer to Jesus. I can't be bitter about it."

Wrapped in a hug before another word could be said, Hope clung to Josh as her throat tightened and heart felt so full it would burst. She could hear his heart beating under her ear on his chest, as fast as her own. His arms tightened around her, and she heard him sigh. Nestled against him, a wistful smile upon her face, Hope almost forgot where she was and what time it was. When he pulled back and inclined his head towards the church, Hope felt her dream state clear and she drew in a long breath.

"You know things will be a little different now." Hope tilted her head.

Josh took her hands again. "How do you mean?"

"I have an interview for a mission trip with Adventist Volunteers on Monday. If that goes well, I'll be applying for more. So there will be times I'm away on mission work. Some short term trips, some long term. But that comes first."

Hope steeled herself against what she was sure was coming. That might be the deal-breaker. She might lose him again. But she now knew who she was and what she wanted to do—at last— and she knew she didn't need a man beside her to do it. That'd just be a bonus.

God you are first. Help me live like you are …

After what seemed like a long silence, Josh raised one of her hands to his mouth and kissed the back of her hand. "I wouldn't expect anything less. In fact, you saying that confirms what I've been feeling of late. Whatever has happened within you, I want to know more. I find myself drawn to you more now than ever."

Hope looked down, her mind a flurry of thankful praises. With a toss of her hair, she looked back up at him. "Not to sound corny, but it's not me you're drawn to. That'd be Jesus."

Josh played with her fingers before looking towards the church. "I kind of figured that. Maybe you could introduce me to Him?"

Hope bit her lip through a smile. This moment was one she'd prayed about, fantasied about, dreamed about, and here it was. She could scarcely believe it ... but then, God was always good. If possible, her world brightened all the more and she threw her arms around Josh, loving the way he drew her up to her tip toes in a full body hug.

Josh felt like home. Always had.

"I would love to." Her voice broke and she hugged him all the tighter. Wonder filled her mind as she slipped back to her feet. Her heart was so full of happiness she was sure it would burst. Josh took her hand and walked her toward church as the worship team began the opening hymns.

God, you are so good. I cannot express with words how happy or thankful I am, I'm just grinning like a fool. How can I ever show you or tell you how much I love you, how thankful I am to you?

As they reached the front doors, Josh let go of her hand and opened the door for her. If he was nervous, it didn't show, but there was no way she could hide the joy that was bubbling through her bloodstream and sending tingles along her skin.

As she stepped past Josh and into the church, she felt his hand enclose around hers once more and an unmistakable impression cleared all other thoughts in her mind.

Worship Me.

SHORT BIBLE
STUDY: HOPE.

1. Dave said to the leaders: "Sometimes we are the only Bible others will read." How does your "Bible" read to the people watching you?

2. Why is it important to consider our actions? Should what we do, and what we say, be the same?

3. Dave suggested Hope read several Bible verses: Psalms 37:4 and Matthew 6:33. What do they mean to you?

4. In chapter 34, Hope makes a significant discovery about herself. Look up Ephesians 2:10 and write down what comes to mind as you think over this verse. Is it significant to you?

5. Can you recall a time when something happened which you couldn't explain, which helped or saved or encouraged you?

A NOTE FROM
THE AUTHOR

The SHAPE program mentioned in this book, is an initiative of the Seventh-Day Adventist Church and has been referenced with permission. If you would like to know more about the program, please see **www.discoveryourshape.org**

The Adventist Volunteers Organisation has been referenced with permission and details relating to their programs can be found at **www.adventistvolunteers.org**

Also, the 16 personalities have been referenced with permission. For more information, please see their website: **www.16personalities.com**

I hope that you have enjoyed this book, and it is my prayer for every reader that you will hear and follow the calling of God in your life, and to never forget: *'For we are God's handiwork, created in Christ Jesus to do good works, which God prepared in advance for us to do.'* Ephesians 2:10.

ACKNOWLEDGEMENTS

First, I would like to thank the Lord God above for inspiring me to write this series, for guiding me and my testimony through the pages of these books to show the goodness of God and the power of prayer in all circumstances.

There have been countless drafts that preceded this final copy and a heart full of thanks goes out to those who have come around me in helping guide and direct the vision for this book in each of its stages. My incredible brothers and sisters in Christ who also moonlight as fantastic proofreaders have been an enormous blessing: Karen O, Karen R, Kate M, Bill M, Nina M, Suzie M, Rose M, Patricia A, and Wayne G.

Patricia Antas, our meeting was God ordained! Thanks to Victor Kulakov for information and guidance regarding the SHAPE program, and Rose Miranda for your information and guidance with Adventist Volunteers.

Nicole Danswan of Initiate Media, once again you've done an incredible artwork for the cover of the third book of this series. And the team at Ark House for putting my work together. You continue to bring make my dream possible. Thank you!

Iola Goulton of Christian Editing Services, once again your insights, knowledge and humor are thought provoking and I am so thankful to your professionalism in guiding this dream to reality.

And lastly, not forgetting the countless number of dogs who have come through my Dog Grooming Salon, who sat patiently while I groomed them and listened to not only just the outline of my stories, but also the intricacies of dialogue, plot, and character arcs. The encouragement you all provided has been priceless. To them, I say a great big thank you!